Short Story International

Tales by the World's Great Contemporary Writers Presented Unabridged

All selections in
Short Story International
are reprinted full and
unabridged in the author's
own words. Nothing is
added, subtracted,
condensed or rewritten.

Editor
Sylvia Tankel

Associate Editor
Erik Sandberg-Diment

Contributing Editor
John Harr

Assistant Editors
Mildred Butterworth
Arlene Loveless
Kirsten Hammerle

Art Director
Mort Rubenstein

Drawings by
John Groth

Circulation Director
Nat Raboy

Production Director
Ludwig K. Marz

Business Manager
John O'Connor

Publisher
Sam Tankel

Volume 4, Number 19, April 1980. *Short Story International* (USPS 375-970) Copyright © by International Cultural Exchange 1980. Printed in the U.S.A. All rights reserved. Reproduction in whole or in part prohibited. Second-class postage paid at Great Neck, N.Y. 11022 and at additional mailing offices. **Editorial offices: P.O. Box 405, Great Neck, N.Y. 11022.** Enclose stamped, self-addressed envelope with previously published stories submitted for possible reprinting in *Short Story International*. Please note *SSI* does not accept unpublished original manuscripts. One year (six issues) subscription for U.S., U.S. possessions $12, Canada $15, other countries $17. Single copy price $2.95. **For subscriptions and address changes write to *Short Story International*. P.O. Box 13913, Philadelphia, Pa. 19104.** *Short Story International* is published bimonthly by International Cultural Exchange, 6 Sheffield Road, Great Neck, N.Y. 11021. Postmaster please send Form 3579 to P.O. Box 13913, Philadelphia, Pa. 19104.

Note from the Editor

Our mail from readers is read as carefully as manuscripts. Much of it proclaims the short story inherently satisfying—in tune with today's tempo. You don't have to commit a large chunk of time, as with a novel, to reach the denouement of a short story.

The following letter from Mr. Roy Parmenter puts it well, and is a paean of praise we're happy to share. (Naturally, with the volume of mail we receive, not all letters are encomiums.)

I had a delightful lunch this noon with Woody Allen (and Kugelmass, Persky, Emily and Daphne). [SSI No. 17.] Just now, thinking how much more fun that was than staring at people in the cafeteria (which is also fun), I thought, "Why not tell them?"

So I am. Telling you how much I enjoyed that story. How much I have enjoyed all of your issues since I began taking SSI. And, how much I look forward to opening the latest issue tonight at home.

You do what must be a very difficult job of finding good stories and choosing the best very well—time after time after time.

For that, thank you.

I only wish your magazine were twice as thick and came twice as often. The only sad part is when I realize I have read every one.

Again, thank you.

Roy Parmenter
Kansas City, Missouri

Our deep thanks to Mr. Parmenter and to all other readers who take the time to comment to us about SSI.

Copyrights
and acknowledgments

We wish to express deep thanks to the authors, publishers, translators and literary agents for their permission to reprint the stories in this issue.

"False Limits" by Vlady Kociancich appeared in *Mundus Artium*, Vol. III, No. 3. English translation by Norman Thomas di Giovanni in collaboration with the author. Reprinted with permission of *Mundus Artium*. "In the Factory" by Graham Sheil was first published by the Eaglehawk Festival of Arts. Copyright 1977 Graham Sheil. "Forsaking All Others" by Beatrice Fines first appeared in *The Saturday Evening Post* Reprinted with permission by The Saturday Evening Post Company © 1972. "Through the Tunnel" by Doris Lessing. Originally published in *The New Yorker*. Copyright © 1955 Doris Lessing; from *The Habit of Loving*, Thomas Y. Crowell, Publishers, N.Y. Copyright © 1957 Doris Lessing. Reprinted with permission of Thomas Y. Crowell, Publishers and Curtis Brown Ltd, London. "Sparring Partners" by Ian Searle originally appeared in *Blackwood's Magazine*, 1978. Reprinted by permission of the author and editor of *Blackwood's*, Edinburgh, 1978. "Imaginary Monologue" by Günter Kunert from *Die Beerdigung findet in aller Stille statt*, © 1968 Carl Hanser Verlag, Munchen-Wien. English translation by Peter E. Firchow and Evelyn S. Firchow appeared in *Hammer and Pen: East German Short Stories*, published by Twayne Publishers, 1979. Reprinted by permission of Carl Hanser Verlag and G.K. Hall and Company. "Domino" by Sujatha Bala Subramanian appeared in *Illustrated Weekly of India*. Copyright © 1978 Sujatha Bala Subramanian. "The Decline and Fall of Our Local Mosque" by A.A. Navis *From Surabaya to Armageddon*, edited and translated by Harry Aveling. English translation © 1976 Heinemann Educational Books (Asia) Ltd. Reprinted by permission. "Disgrace" by Gideon Telpaz. English translation first appeared in *Present Tense* 1978. English translation © 1978 Gideon Telpaz. "Unacceptable Mixture" by Leopoldo Chariarse from *The Custom House of Desire*. Translation by J.H. Matthews. Copyright 1975 The Regents of the University of California. Reprinted by permission of the University of California Press. "Stresspoint" by Colin Beadon first appeared in *London Magazine*. Copyright © 1978 Colin Beadon. "Eccentric Ferns" by Peter Nazareth first appeared in *Dhana*, Uganda. Copyright Peter Nazareth. "The Future of Little Banana" by Kevin Costello first appeared in *Event*, Vol. 4, No. 2, Canada. Reprinted by permission. "When Money Talked to Me" by Roy Wolper first appeared in *The Texas Quarterly*. Copyright 1966 *The Texas Quarterly*. "Guests from the Province" by Arkady Rovner. Translation by Elisavietta Ritchie. English translation first appeared in *Confrontation*. Copyright 1975 Arkady Rovner.

Photo credits: Doris Lessing © Peter Lessing. Günter Kunert © Wolfgang Fischer. Peter Nazareth by Mark Locke.

Table of Contents

9   **Argentina**   **Vlady Kociancich** False Limits

17   **Australia**   **Graham Sheil** In the Factory

29   **Canada**   **Beatrice Fines** Forsaking All Others

41   **England**   **Doris Lessing** Through the Tunnel

53   **England**   **Ian Searle** Sparring Partners

65   **Germany**   **Günter Kunert** Imaginary Monologue

77   **India**   **Sujatha Bala Subramanian** Domino

85   **Indonesia**   **A.A. Navis** The Decline and Fall
of Our Local Mosque

93   **Israel**   **Gideon Telpaz** Disgrace

107   **Peru**   **Leopoldo Chariarse** Unacceptable Mixture

117   **Trinidad**   **Colin Beadon** Stresspoint

127   **Uganda**   **Peter Nazareth** Eccentric Ferns

133   **USA**   **Kevin Costello** The Future of Little Banana

145   **USA**   **Roy Wolper** When Money Talked to Me

157   **USSR**   **Arkady Rovner** Guests from the Province

"The atmosphere of the house,
the forced secrecy of horror, shattered
Elisa's innocent words."

False Limits

BY VLADY KOCIANCICH

Changing positions in a troubled marriage.

HE would write a letter because to see his best friend and tell him
face to face was impossible. He had often thought about speaking
to him but never quite could; he imagined Enrique's face, the way
his expression would change, his look of astonishment, his inter-
ruptions ("But it can't be—are you sure?"), which would force
him to explain or perhaps excuse himself or at worst confess that it
had only been a joke.

Up to now it had never occurred to him that friendship and love
are, in certain cases, proofs of a helpless solitude. He could not
face Enrique because Enrique would not understand. Someone
not so close to him would have been better. He thought, if I had
such a friend I'd tell him everything. But Enrique was so loyal, so
good, that it was impossible to utter a word to him. Writing him
might keep up the illusion of an understanding between them and
at the same time give Enrique a chance to think over his reply, to

weigh carefully each reason he would use to convince him he had been dreaming.

He didn't think the letter would be enough, but as an introduction it would at least spare him Enrique's looks of expectancy and bewilderment. He hesitated, and while hesitating—out of an impulse that ran contrary to his will—he was writing: "It's about my wife." He filled the letter with labored sentences, with excuses, with evasions, and with justifications. Suddenly he stopped and looked around. He was alone. He was peacefully surrounded by everyday things, as if nothing had really happened. He read: "It's about my wife. It's about Elisa. She's not ill, nor is there another man mixed up in this. . . ." Denying, he could go on forever. Enrique would never find out the truth. Still roundabout in his approach, he gave one last trite explanation before getting down to the facts: "It's very hard to make certain things clear to outsiders, because to a married couple that's what others are—outsiders. How idiotic to think love unites. How sentimental. Two people living together stand as if on different planes, most of which are secret. I won't try explaining anything to you because I don't know myself what's happened, but here are the facts . . ."

He stopped again. He had heard a noise behind him, the shuffle of slippers on the rug. Quickly he covered the letter with the first thing he could lay his hands on—a map of greater Buenos Aires—and began studying it: Adrogué, Lomas de Zamora, familiar routes . . . He pronounced these names to himself, trying to escape Elisa and the silence, which was so obvious it was almost like another person in the room. But also, though he did not lift his eyes from the map, he listened hard for the faint sound of Elisa's approaching steps. Then, unable to bear it any longer, he called without turning around, "Elisa?"

"Yes?" Her voice was neutral, with the sweetness of utter indifference.

"Nothing—except that I'm going out."

"Oh."

"Do you want anything from town?" he asked, obedient to his old habit of adding a word or two when he felt guilty.

"No."

He got up hurriedly, relieved by her answer, which excused him from having to come back right away. He gathered up his papers, the letter among them, put everything into a leather briefcase, and, feeling both stupid and afraid, left for his office.

Of course, he did not mail the letter. He kept it in a pocket for several days, transferring it from one suit to another, but he never mailed it. At last Enrique rang him up, wondering why they had not been getting together for drinks. Elisa had spoken to him; she was surprised too. She said he was too old to break his habit of meeting Enrique either on Wednesday nights or Thursdays before seven. Elisa always teased him about his way of organizing his habits with the same thoroughness he applied to his work at the office. This time her remark sounded to him like mockery. The atmosphere of the house, the forced secrecy of horror, shattered Elisa's innocent words.

Up to that moment he had fought against all sorts of troubles and out of these battles he had emerged victorious; this had led him to believe that one of his rock bottom virtues was strength. Yes, he considered himself strong, able to face anything, even the worst situations, but how could he understand this madness which surrounded him now—in spite of the sensibleness of all his past acts and the smooth way his days had run—without any apparent cause?

A man like him does not become disturbed overnight; he waits to see what will happen and then takes the plunge into analysis. This had been his first impulse. At the very moment Elisa changed, he had thought, I must see an analyst.

He would call Enrique to find out if he knew a good one—not one of those clowns who organize LSD sessions, of course, but a sensible doctor, an understanding listener. As a listener, Enrique would have done well, but, preferring the impersonality of science, he never once spoke to him. He waited. And while postponing the moment of coming to grips with his problem, he tried to imagine a dialogue which might begin in this way:

"It's about my wife."

The analyst would not risk any conclusions, he would let him talk.

"I never noticed anything strange about her. She's a silent, quiet woman. But her character—Elisa herself—has nothing to do with what's happening to me. She's outside all this."

That was exactly why he could not talk to her. He stopped himself to ask if it had been always this way—Elisa distant from him, he trapped in his own silence, both of them avoiding the mention of anything unpleasant or dangerous. They'd had such a peaceful life.

"Elisa and I never had a quarrel—well, maybe once. Yes, now I remember, years ago we once had a fight, but I don't know what about. Yesterday, while we were having breakfast, I noticed that Elisa had no hands. Or maybe she did, maybe I just couldn't see them. No hands. She was sitting there as usual, but without hands."

He would stop to watch the doctor's reaction, but the doctor would display an impassive face so as not to lose his fee for subsequent visits. He would ask, very politely, "And what else?"

"I behaved as though nothing had happened. I tried to think—I still believe in this possibility—that it was only an hallucination, fatigue, overwork, my eyes."

That first day had been more uncomfortable than anything else. He denied the change in her with all his strength and with less courage than would have been required to take it lightly, at the same time piling explanation on explanation—his fatigue, his vision.

This visit to the doctor was so real that he decided not to see him. He told himself that what he wanted was an answer, not theories. Elisa without hands was a terrifying sight but still bearable, since she had not lost them in an accident (there were no traces of blood or of torn flesh). It was like the lingering remnants of a nightmare, and one easily grows used to nightmares, so long as they don't make much sense. At some point later on, weakened by fear and sorrow, he wondered why he had not immediately run out of the house instead of trying to grow gradually accustomed to the horror.

This attitude of well-mannered acceptance lasted till the moment Elisa's eyes disappeared. She had lifted her empty face to him for its morning kiss, and he stepped back instinctively for the door. Moving clumsily in his fear, he got into his car, the keys clinking together in his trembling hand, and started the motor. Then a neighbor, a face he did not bother to identify, was approaching him, wanting to be helped with his car, which had gone dead or had sunk into a soft shoulder or something of the kind. As at the outer limits of a nightmare, he was held back by this series of efforts he was forced to make against his will and by his neighbor's small talk, all the while feeling Elisa's empty stare at the back of his head. But he did not see a doctor, nor did he mail the letter to Enrique. He only thought about escaping. It might have been a sensible decision not to return home. But he could not leave. That would have meant confronting Elisa and explaining why he was leaving her. And where would he go? He put forward these and other excuses so as not to have to admit the inexplicable feeling tying him to his home and his wife. All he did was shut himself up in his work. There was no detail into which he did not enter, no meeting he did not attend. His colleagues seemed not to mind, but were somewhat taken aback when he began meddling in the affairs of others. Now he was coming home very late; he would stay on at the office or at a bar, hoping on his return to find Elisa asleep.

Not wanting to wake her, he avoided turning on the lights. He would then grope for the bed and lie with his back to her, in one corner, like an angry child.

For a long time, for nearly a month, he let himself go on living in his nightmare, leaving home early each morning and coming back late at night. Not so late as to arouse Elisa's suspicions, however, but late enough to find her already asleep. With a glance at her side of the bed he could vaguely make out her head, a large spot of golden hair on the pillow. He would then be tempted to put his arms around her, not out of love but out of desperation, driven by a need to do something—anything. But he huddled in fear on his side of the bed and pulled the sheets over his head.

During the day, in a rush of endless tasks, he tried to forget his wife's gradual disappearance, but Elisa, handless, eyeless, like a broken doll, often broke into the conversation when he was lunching with other people, and made his blood run cold. He began to take little notice of his behavior. He was no longer able to cover up his fear before others and would stop a moment before any door and pray not to have Elisa open it for him.

He endured his nights stoically, sure there was no way of avoiding them, and, out of desperation, always managed to sleep. He had not had a single sleepless night, but in his dreams he found himself with Elisa. Once, he had cried out in his sleep and she stirred. He held his breath, rigid on his side of the bed. He heard her softly saying; "Are you all right? What is it?"

Close to tears in his fright, he begged her to go on sleeping, assuring her that he was perfectly all right. She turned her back to him without another word. They never talked again.

Now it was no more a matter of seeing an analyst or waiting for Enrique's advice. He had passed the limits of one nightmare and was entering into another, as if a last door had been closed on him. Motionless at the edge of the bed, knowing that if he stirred or got up she would come after him, he imagined the color of her hair in the dark. It was the only thing about her he still remembered.

He began to weep silently, while striking up an imaginary dialogue with his wife.

"Elisa, what's happening to us?"

He saw himself and Elisa in a trap, two figures drawn by the same hand, making up part of who knew what bewildering picture.

He began to regret the long-past time when they were both open and things were clear and they loved each other. With the certainty that nothing could now save him from his present horror, admitting for the first time that no tomorrow would come, all at once he understood everything. Violently, desperately frightened, he turned toward Elisa's incomplete body to take her in his arms, to try to hold together what little was left of her, feeling that this is what he should have done that first time. But there on the pillow lay nothing but a lock of golden hair, and in a matter of moments it too disappeared.

"These are the facts, Enrique," he wrote. "Elisa's gone. I can hear her. If I were to touch her, I could feel her skin; sometimes, when I brush against her, I can hear her breath. If she didn't exist, if she were really dead, I don't think it would matter to me. But living with her this way is unbearable and living without her is impossible. I have not gone back to work. I'm telling you all this without pain or fear because I have no other fate than to remain here. I care for nothing in this world but Elisa."

"Raúl."

It was his wife's voice calling him after such a long time. He got up from the desk, turned, and saw her. Elisa once again, Elisa tall, whole, beautiful, watching him with a grave look in her eyes, while he dared not speak for fear of breaking the spell of this new dream. He was trembling and had to support himself against the desk.

It took him an eternity to come back to life. It meant just that—to be living again in this small, simple world of manageable troubles, troubles shared with others. He would never be alone again.

When he came to his senses, to the almost unbearable happiness of being himself again, he heard Elisa explaining to him, perhaps for the fifth time, "I'm sorry, Raúl, but I'm leaving. I'm in love with another man."

Vlady Kociancich was born 1942 in Buenos Aires and studied at the University of Buenos Aires. Her stories appear in literary journals and in her own collections. Norman Thomas di Giovanni translated the story in collaboration with the author.

"It was then I'd begun to wonder:
if I stayed at the factory, would I become
like Norm?"

In the Factory

BY GRAHAM SHEIL

Financial security . . . what price?

I pedaled fast on the smooth bitumen of the main road, swerved
'round a parked car and a driver blared his horn at me. I jerked my
thumb and shouted he needn't think I was gunna dent his new
Customline! I was still nettled over the argument I'd had that
morning. With my parents. The same argument as last week and
the week before and before that. There was *security* at the factory,
they'd said; there was *opportunity*; I ought to be grateful I could
stay!

But it was really myself I was sore at; I was pedaling to the
factory this morning, as I had each weekday morning for the past
thirteen months, because of my inability to make up my mind.

And, yes-s-s-s, because of Caroline.

I braked, turned, rode up the open-drain center of the paving-
stone lane beside the factory and in through the loading door.
There was gray-white dust thick on the concrete floor and the bags

full of clay, asbestos and "earth" stacked everywhere; when rain or wind hit the iron roof, dust fell from the rafters.

I rode between the bags and the machinery to where Norm was shoveling coke into one of the ovens, and swore at the dust the tires threw up over the bike.

"Now, now, we'll have none of that language," Norm said.

He was taking off on Mr. Arnold. He didn't do the Mr. Arnold bit very well, but he chortled to himself whenever he did it. Norm was over fifty, I suppose; short and made even shorter by a stoop. He wore the clothes he always wore: a worn-out-at-elbows jumper and a dilapidated felt hat with its frosting of white dust.

I hoisted bike to shoulder and made a show of hurrying to the change-room. The argument with my parents had kept me late. Not that Mr. Arnold would know, as he was never there before nine, but in some indefinable way it emphasized my relationship to him. He was my uncle. The day I began working there he told me it would be as well if I addressed him as the others did, and I'd told him that was all right by me.

Firebrick and Insulations Ltd was a jumble of buildings with a showroom that faced the main road, then an office, two change-rooms, a yard with just sufficient space to walk between stacked and rusting machinery on either side of a path that connected to the factory itself. During the war more than a dozen hands had been employed; now there was just Norm, Stef and myself.

I returned from the change-room to find Norm had both ovens alight. This was really my job, so I made amends by preparing "his" brickmaking machine. Cleaning the rollers, painting them with oil, cleaning and painting the table where the solid rectangular blocks of "compo" were forced from the machine, across rollers, to be cut by wires into insulating bricks.

Norm had worked that same machine since before the war. Over twenty-six years, when you added them up. Once I'd told him of the arguments with my parents, and he'd told me when he was younger he'd decided to leave the factory. He had made up his mind, had looked up the 'papers and seen there were job offerings and had told his wife. Then he came to work and afterwards to the pub, same as he always did.—But you'd made up your mind!—I'd said. Norm had just grinned and shrugged . . .

It was then I'd begun to wonder: if I stayed at the factory, would I become like Norm?

Or Stef?

Stef worked the crusher at the far end of the factory. The thick fog of dust there was proof Stef had been at work for some time. For hours, perhaps. He lived in the flat above the factory's office, which he seldom left even at weekends. And he often started the crusher at seven or earlier, yet he never knocked-off early to make up. Some Monday mornings we would find he had been crushing at weekends.

When Norm came to set and tighten the wires on the cutter and to screw down grease-cups, I wheeled the handtruck to Stef's end of the factory. Up close the clatter of crusher blades was deafening. Within the dust-fog Stef was visible only as a vague blur attached to the side of the crusher.

I hefted three half-bags of "earth" onto the truck, wheeled them to Norm, then back for another load. Four loads of "earth," two of clay, one of asbestos. Norm already had the mixer going. He stood drawing on one of the roll-y'-owns he smoked while jets squirted water and the mixer blades stirred the powdered clay, "earth" and asbestos into "compo." I wiped my nose on my shirt sleeves and snorted out the dust already congealing there. Thank God Stef was only crushing clay! Clay is heavy and its dust did not spread far from the crusher but "earth," diatomaceous earth, is light and dry and crushes into a powder that hung in the factory like a dense fog, blurring sight and sound, clogging nostrils and penetrating clothes. Somewhere in the factory was a dustmask that was presented whenever an inspector called. I had never seen it used. When the dust was bad we tied calico strips around our faces and blew dust from our nostrils as best we could.

Norm had tipped "compo" from the mixer and had the machine going and I was carting bricks to the racks, when Stef passed. He said nothing, just nodded as he always did.

I grinned to Norm. He grinned back. He held up one finger, and waited till Stef was beyond hearing.

"One!"

Mr. Arnold must have had deliveries to make, because by ten o'clock *smoko* we had seen neither him nor the office girl, Caroline. Before *smoko,* though, Stef had passed us again, and we had again waited until he was beyond hearing, grinned, then said together:

"Two!"

Every day we counted the number of times he passed us. We called him *The Cricketer* and referred to his trips as "runs." If he made more than a dozen "runs" in a day we'd say he was "batting well," or "in good form," that day. Those days he was "batting well" were days when he was crushing "earth" and the dust-fog was thick through all the factory. He always returned smelling faintly of something sweet, and humming.

During *smoko* Norm and I sat on half-full bags near the ovens, which was that part of the factory furthest from the crusher. Norm drank tea and read the 'paper. I had a book but did not read it. I was hoping Caroline would come to see if we wanted anything for lunch.

Not long after I began working at the factory, Caroline let me take her to the pictures one Saturday night. We sat in the dark of the back stalls where all the kids with their birds sat. As soon as the lights went down, a couple in front started cuddling and on either side there were giggles and whispered arguments. At first I thought I might hold Caroline's hand, perhaps even put my arm around her, but then I wondered if she might think that too forward. Unable to make up my mind, I did nothing. I watched Spencer Tracy being towed out to sea by a giant fish. After interval, the couple in front sank down until they were lying along the seat and those on either side kept looking down and giggling. Afterwards I bought Caroline a malted milk and walked her home. I told her it was one of the best films I'd seen. She said she didn't know why *any*one 'ud wanna watch a film about a *fish*! The next Monday, at the factory, she said I was a nong. I said, Whatayamean—a nong? She said I didn't know anything, that was all. The following Saturday she started going to drive-ins with a clerk who got a lend of his brother's car.

I was beginning to work up some excuse for going to the office, when Caroline came flouncing between the stacked machinery and bags of clay.

"Anythin' t'day?" she asked, poised with pencil and notepad.

"I'll have whatever that clerk that takes you to drive-ins gets," I said.

Norm chortled. Caroline looked at me smugly.

"Wouldn't you like t' know!" she said. "An' he's not a clerk—he's a trainee-teller."

"Must be a big fella," I said, "t' be able t' hold up a pen all day. He'll end up with a hernia from it."

"That's a disgusting thing t' say!—Whatta you want, Norm? Since he can only talk dirty."

Norm said he wanted nothin' t'day. Thanks.

"An' whattabout you, Nong-head?"

"Told y'."

"Then you'll get nothin'."

"I'll have a pint o' milk."

"Get it y'self!"

"It's your job!"

"Y' c'n just get it y'self—Foul-mouth!"

She turned and walked away with her stiff-at-the-knees, deliberately hip-jiggling, walk. I watched until she turned from sight behind rusting machinery.

"Now, now, we'll have no naughty thoughts," Norm said. Then, no longer taking off on Mr. Arnold, he said that girl sure had me on a collar-'n'-chain.

He stood and threw tea-dregs onto the cokes in the nearest oven, as Stef passed us, humming.

"Three!"

Unlike Stef, Norm never drank during the day. At five to five he filled his kettle and put it on the cokes in the oven; at five he splashed water from the kettle into a basin, washed just his face and hands, changed, then hurried out the loading door, headed for the pub. Though the pub was half a mile away, Norm boasted he'd never got there later than a quarter past in his life!

Norm set the machine going; I went for another load of clay. Stef's shape detached itself from the side of the crusher and came towards me, coughing. He jerked his thumb in the direction of the crusher and said something I could not hear above the din. He brought his mouth close to my ear and shouted "Blocked!" A blockage was cleared by prodding an iron rod between the beaters, which often caught it, flinging the rod crazily and often slamming him across the hand or forearm. Stef coughed, spat, then resignedly moved back to become part of the solid blur of the crusher.

A day when there were blockages was a day when his score of "runs" was high.

I wheeled the half-bags to the brick-making machine, to find Norm talking to Mr. Arnold. On seeing me, Mr. Arnold said:

"Now, now, boy, you start stamping. Norm's got enough bags."

"He'll need more clay," I said.

Mr. Arnold said it'd be a change if I did as I was told *when* I was told.

"Well he *needs* clay!"

Mr. Arnold looked up at the rafters as though he had not heard, and started humming.

When I wheeled the handtruck back to the crusher, I could not see Stef; though above the din, I heard him coughing. Stef had worked at the factory since he'd come from Europe as a young man, and I wondered how he'd survived thirty years of breathing dust eight or nine hours each day. Lately his bouts of coughing had become more frequent, and there were more days when he was "batting well" and his score of "runs" was over the dozen.

I dumped that load of half-bags next to the mixer; then cleaned and painted oil on the faces of the stamping machine, put the first brick on the machine's raised platform, swung down the big counterweighted iron wheel, and the stamping face hit the brick compressing it into the mould through which the platform had dropped. I swung the wheel down hard, once, twice, then back up.

"Now, now, boy," Mr. Arnold said. "You go at it too hard."

Mr. Arnold was thin and would have been tall were he not also stooped; he wore a gray dust-coat. He said he'd give me a hand with the bricks, and began carting those I stamped to the drying racks and bringing unstamped ones. While I stamped bricks, he stood behind me, humming.

Other than my parents and his wife, I was Mr. Arnold's only relative. It was understood I was to learn the business by working there, then later, when he retired, I would take over the running of it. My parents spoke of it as my *Great Opportunity*. And, even I acknowledged, for a kid who'd left school at fifteen, it *was* a great opportunity.

Yet there were times I wondered: if I stayed at the factory and I did become boss here, would I become like Mr. Arnold?

I punched bricks, getting more and more depressed by Mr. Arnold's humming, and Mr. Arnold getting more and more fidgety. When Caroline came stepping between the bags and called Mr. Arnold was wanted on the 'phone, I saw he was as relieved as I was.

By the time five to twelve came and Norm went to put his kettle on, Stef had made his fifth and sixth "runs" for the day, and Norm and I had counted them aloud.

I left Norm to read his newspaper beside the ovens and took my lunch and book to sit in the back of Mr. Arnold's utility truck parked in the lane. I settled myself so as to have the warmth of sun on my body, but could hold the book in shadow. I opened at the dog-eared page to read of battles fought with boots and staves of wood and the burning of farm houses in the apple orchards of California. After a few pages I lost interest in the strife of fruit-pickers, and searched among earlier chapters, reading a paragraph in one place, and two or three in another, where days spent picking in the orchards were described. Each day began with frost, then cold winds blowing among the rows of trees, later there was calm and afternoon sun. The picking, carrying buckets of apples between rows to the checkers and sorters, the comradeship of the pickers, all seemed very clean, somehow, after the morning in the factory . . . Beyond the outer suburbs were cherry orchards where picking would begin soon, then peaches would come in; there would be grape picking after Christmas. I thought of myself up a ladder among foliage and sky, filling buckets with cherries, and wondered whether Caroline would fit in with the sky and foliage picture.

Just then she came towards me from the loading door: pronged sweater, scissor steps, holding something behind her.

"What d' y' think I've got?"

I thought of answering, The Sack! or, A ring from the clerk-jerk t' say he'd got another bird! or something smart like that. But before I could say a thing, she produced from behind her back a bottle of milk.

"There!" she said. "You don't deserve it, but."

"You were scared I'd tell my uncle you wouldn't—that's why. You'd be fresh out of a job."

Though my relationship to Mr. Arnold was never spoken of with Stef or Norm, I made sure Caroline got the message.

"Fat lot o' notice he takes of you," she said.

"Or you!"

"Ohhh, I get 'round him." She was being Miss Smug.

"One day I'll be boss here. Then you'll 've had it."

"Huuh!"

The bit about me being boss was another message I made sure Caroline got. I thought it might impress. After all, Mr. Arnold had married one of his office girls.

"I'll be boss here, awright," I said. "So y' just better watch it."

"You!" She turned and walked away with her hip-jiggling walk. She knew I was watching. "You the boss," she flung the words over her shoulder. "Big deal!"

Yet she was impressed: I could tell. Norm could say what he liked about a collar-'n'-chain; she did keep leading me on. And it was the one-day-I'll-be-boss-here bit that kept her at least that interested.

I sat in the tray of the truck, drinking the milk and thinking about Caroline, until Norm called from the loading door that if I had no intention of working that afternoon it was all right with him.

Through the afternoon I carted and dumped half-bags for Norm, carted and punched bricks and set them to dry on racks. Together Norm and I counted Stef's "runs." After Stef's ninth "run" Norm came across from his machine and said there'd been

IN THE FACTORY

an ad' in the 'paper for laborers to work at setting out and looking after lawns and public gardens. I asked if he was going to apply. Norm said he was past changing now. I slammed the stamper down hard. If he wasn't going to apply what was the point of even thinking about it?

Norm had shrugged and returned to his machine when Mr. Arnold called to him from down by the ovens. Norm switched off his machine, and made a show of hurrying. Mr. Arnold seemed agitated. He spoke hurriedly to Norm, who seemed not to comprehend, then hurried back toward the office with Norm scurrying after him.

I carted and stamped one pile of bricks, then another. Neither Norm, Mr. Arnold, or Stef had returned. Stef's crusher began making an odd grating sound, so I went and switched it off, then walked between the bags and the rusting machinery to the office. Only Caroline was there.

"Oh you," she said. "You don't know what's happened." She was trying to be Miss Smug again, but with less success. She was a frightened little girl, and she began talking very rapidly.

"There was this bang on the stairs. See? And I went and looked and told Mr. Arnold, 'Stef's fallen down the stairs and he's just lying.' Mr. Arnold said he expected he'd get up in a minute. But he didn't. Then I went and looked again. Mr. Arnold came too and went up the stairs. He came back and said, 'Just go on with yer typing, girl,' and ran out the door t' get Norm. But he'd only just got through the door an' he's back. 'Ring a doctor, girl,' he said. So I did. But what for? Anyone could see he was dead!"

There were footsteps on the stairs. Mr. Arnold and a squat, wild-gray-haired man in a crumpled suit and carrying a small case, stood at the bottom of the stairs without speaking to each other. They looked as though they'd already said anything that could be said between them.

After a while, Mr. Arnold said:

"Now, now, surely all this isn't necessary. I mean, there are no relatives, not even friends. I can assure you of that, and a post-mortem will just . . . well, there's no necessity, surely . . ."

The squat man in the crumpled suit looked at Mr. Arnold as

though he'd told him and told him and just wasn't going to tell him again. He turned to Caroline.

"Miss, you'd better ring the police."

Caroline was standing one hand on hip.

"What'll I say?"

"Tell them . . ." He looked across to Mr. Arnold. "It doesn't matter. I'll ring from back at the surgery."

The doctor left, and Mr. Arnold trod heavily back up the stairs.

For a time I just stood there. Then I went to the foot of the stairs.

"Ooooooh," Caroline said. "Y're not goin' up?"

At the top of the stairs the door was open with Mr. Arnold and Norm inside. Mr. Arnold standing by one side of the door, Norm by the other. On a couch behind and between them, two gray blankets outlined Stef's profile. And high on a wall above where Stef lay, was a big, round, wind-up-from-the-bottom clock.

Norm had turned to gaze up at the clock. He said it was all very well f' that doctor t' say he'd better stay. He didn't have to stand 'round waiting till the police made up their minds t' come. It was a quarter t' five already, an' he'd never in his life b'fore been later than a quarter past. Never!

Mr. Arnold looked up at the ceiling and said it wasn't as if Stef had a family or anything. No doubt a post-mortem would show *some* dust or asbestos on Stef's lungs. People always get t' hear of these things; and he'd always been, he said, respectable.

I walked quietly about the room. Besides the couch there was a table and just one chair; a curtain divided from the rest of the room a washbasin and gas ring on top of a cupboard. Port bottles were stacked along one wall from the cupboard to the doorway into the bedroom. The bottles were stacked two deep and shoulder high.

Standing by the couch, I looked at Mr. Arnold and Norm. Between them they had worked more than half a century of years with Stef; yet one was looking forlornly at the clock, the other with his brow worried into folds by what might be said. I realized I too felt no loss or sorrow for Stef, only a curiosity as to whether he looked different, now he was dead.

I reached for a corner of the blanket and saw Norm give a quick shake of his head and Mr. Arnold abruptly put up his hand as though to stop me.

Somehow I'd expected him to look different. But he looked the same down to the white dust in his hair and among the stubble on his chin.

Looking down at him, searching for some change, I became aware of the clock ticking. This sound came to me as the counting out of the seconds of my own life, as the seconds had been counted out of Stef's. I let the blanket fall, then turned to stand looking from Norm on one side of the door to Mr. Arnold on the other and back again. Neither of them had looked at the dead man. And I knew then that my future life at the factory would move only in the narrow space between those two.

Abruptly I passed between them, down the stairs to the office. Caroline was speaking into the 'phone. I heard her say she just bet he didn't have a clue what'd happened here.

In the change-room I left my jumper and overalls on the floor in their halo of dust and swung the bike to my shoulder; I strode, not to the factory and the loading door, but straight out the front, leaving footprints of white on the showroom linoleum.

Caroline looked startled. She said into the 'phone he could hang-on if he wanted, then banged the 'phone down on the desk.

"Isn't knock-off time yet," she complained. Then, crossing with her hip-jiggling walk to me, she said:

"Knockin'-off early, eh? Think we're boss here already do we?"

"Not me," I said.

"But will be . . . What y' doin' Sat'day night, Hughy?"

I said *she* was going with the clerk-jerk.

"Wel-l-l-l a girl *could* change her mind," she said. "He's on the 'phone now, ringin' me up t' tell me his brother wants the car. An' after he'd promised . . . I told him straight if he couldn't even keep a promise I knew someone who could."

I swung the bike down to the floor and reached for the door-knob.

"Thought y' liked me," she said.

I opened the door and stooped to tuck trousers into socks. Behind me I heard Caroline stomp heels-down-hard to the 'phone and say into it there was a kid here tryin' t' big-time by askin' her out. Boy, did she give him the brush-off . . .

I scooted the bike along the footpath, swinging my leg over. There are others, I was thinking. There're plenty of others. Other jobs, too. Jobs in sunlight, jobs with the skill and cunning of hands. But it was not just the sunlight and cleanness I wanted, there was something else. I did not know what it was. It was its lack I was aware of. And the lack was not only in the factory and the people there, it was in myself as well.

I pedaled fast on the smooth bitumen. Faster and faster. I've left, I kept telling myself. I've actually left. And I won't be back.

Born 1938 in Melbourne, Graham Sheil left school at fifteen "to commence my education as laboratory assistant, laborer, apprentice optical mechanic, pick-'n'-shovel miner, bike rider, company representative; and now combine proprietorship of an optical wholesale company and writing." His stories have been published "by just about every one in Australia who publishes short stories." They appear in magazines, newspapers, anthologies and his own collection of short stories. "In the Factory" was the 1977 winner of the Rolfe Bolderwood Short Story Award. Mr. Sheil enjoys his family, his work, Australian history, eating, and traveling on foot.

". . . wagging tongues and curious minds
had discovered a multitude of reasons for
the Mulligans' unusual behavior."

Forsaking All Others

BY BEATRICE FINES

The grace of kindness and friendship.

I first saw the Mulligans one burning hot day in July the year I was
eleven and Maggie was nine. It's long ago now, but I remember
every detail of how it was. That was our second summer in the
Rainy River Valley, and I remember Mother standing tall and
straight in the open doorway of the new squared-log house, with
her skirts pinned up at the sides to keep the hem free of dust.

"Come, fetch me a pail of creek water," she called to Maggie
and me.

She held the pail out, and Maggie ran and took it, swinging it by
the handle.

"Now hold it on its side and let it fill slowly and don't rile the
water," Mother said.

We got water that was clear enough, but the creek flowed
through muskeg, and it was amber, not crystal. We set the pail
upon the bank, hard and brown with drought that year. Then,

holding our skirts and petticoats high, we waded into the creek for a few minutes of sensual delight in its gasping coldness and in the silken feel of mud between our toes. The day was silent and still with heat, and we eased our way along, pushing sluggish, soundless waves ahead of us, absorbed in their changing patterns of light and shadow. After a time we sensed, rather than heard, someone come and stand on the bank above, and looking up, we saw a child, a stranger.

She was three, perhaps four, and elflike, with a small, pointed face and large, solemn dark eyes. She stood perfectly still, hands clasped in front of her faded calico skirt, bare toes curled against the prickly grass. For a moment surprise tongue-tied both Maggie and me, for we got to see our known neighbors seldom enough, and strangers almost never. Then Maggie, always quicker than I, hissed in my ear, "She can be the little girl when we play house!"

She called out a welcoming "Hello," and began to scramble up the bank.

The child did not speak or smile but unclasped her hands, caught the sides of her skirt and retreated a few steps, her eyes never leaving us.

"Don't go away," entreated Maggie. "We want to play with you."

At that moment we heard a man's voice calling, "Nellie, Nellie," and the little girl turned instantly and ran.

When we got to the top of the bank we could see two figures a little distance down the tote road—a man, stocky and square and with a heavy, bearded face, and a woman, slight and frail like the child. They were carrying lard pails, and we knew they must have been up on the rock picking blueberries. Maggie called out "Hello" again and waved her hand, but they turned quite as if they had neither heard nor seen us and, with the child trailing after, disappeared in a twist of the trail. Maggie and I, surprise still weighing our tongues, took our pail of water up to the house in silence, then burst upon Mother with a flood of words.

"I don't know who they might be," Mother mused, pouring the water into a pan for warming. "I haven't heard of anyone coming in, or anyone down the line expecting visitors."

We learned more about the strangers two days later. Father took the wagon and went four miles out the road to Alex Stewart's for flour and tea and the mail.

"Their name's Mulligan," he explained to Mother on his return, "and Stewart says they came in with their stuff piled into the back of an old broken-down democrat behind the sorriest-looking horse he has seen in a lifetime. They gave cash for their groceries, even when he told them he'd give credit till the timber came out in the fall. They've taken Bill McCullough's place."

"That miserable shack?" There was genuine alarm in Mother's voice. "The rats took it over when Bill left!"

"Now Ada, they've all summer to build. This was no palace when we came, remember. Stewart said his wife invited them in for a cup of tea, but Mulligan said no thanks, they'd best be on, and the woman said not a word, but sat staring straight ahead. Most unfriendly, Stewart said. He asked where they come from and Mulligan answered 'back East' without a word more, and cleared out. I think, Ada, we'd do well to just let the Mulligans be."

But Mother was not one to let anyone be. Spurred by her own loneliness and the compassion that was the heartcore of her nature, she baked a pan of buns, and set out along the trail to the McCullough place with Maggie and me tagging along. We'd been there before, in winter bouncing over snow-covered stumps on the stoneboat, in spring picking our way carefully along the edges of water-filled holes. This day the trail was summer-shady and filled with birdsong.

The McCullough shack looked deserted. Weeds grew among the stumps of the little clearing right to the very door. But there was a horse grazing behind the poplar-pole stable and a wisp of smoke rose from the stovepipe that was thrust through the roof. We expected someone to notice us and open the door, but nothing stirred; so Mother tapped lightly and called out. We listened and thought we heard a faint rustling within. Mother tapped again while Maggie and I peered around the sides of the shack and scanned the fringes of the bush. All was silence.

"They must be away picking berries," Mother said at last, and set her pan of buns on the doorstep.

We turned away, but when we reached the spot where the path dipped into the bush I looked back at the window of the lonely little cabin and caught a fleeting glimpse of a tiny pale face.

"Mother!" I grasped her sleeve. "She's there, inside—the little girl!"

But now the window gave an empty stare.

"I'm sure I saw her," I said, denying my own creeping doubt.

Mother shook her head. "You must have imagined it. The sunlight on the window played a trick."

And so, though the image persisted, I could no longer believe it.

That night I lay wakeful in the bed beside Maggie, feeling at once the beating heat from the day-warmed rafters and the cooling evening breeze from the open window. I could hear Mother and Dad speaking softly in their room below, and gradually I became aware that they were talking about the Mulligans. There was a stovepipe hole in the floor, and now, trembling a little with guilt, I crept out of bed and put my ear to it.

"Someone *was* in the cabin," Mother was saying. "I'm sure I heard movement, and then Annie looked back and saw the little girl at the window. I can't understand it, John. Everyone else is so eager to make friends when they come in."

"You might as well forget any notion of making friends of the Mulligans," Dad said. "I was talking to Ben Smythe. His wife went over—walked the whole five miles—and like you, got no answer to her knocking. Then Joe Taylor asked Mulligan to help with his hog slaughtering and got a flat 'no.'"

In a very few weeks, stories of the new family had spread from farm to farm and wagging tongues and curious minds had discovered a multitude of reasons for the Mulligans' unusual behavior.

"The woman and child are both deaf and dumb critters and Mulligan's embarrassed for them."

"The woman's simple minded since the child was born."

"They're living in sin and ashamed to face Christians."

"Mulligan murdered a man Down East. The law's on his trail."

Maggie and I heard all these tales and discussed them in hushed whispers.

"Wouldn't it be awful to be deaf and dumb?"

"The most horriblest thing in the world."

"I bet Mr. Mulligan carries a pistol all the time—him being a criminal."

"We're lucky he didn't shoot us when we went up to the door."

"I wouldn't go up to their door again for anything."

"I might. I would for sure if he wasn't there."

I had to make statements like this sometimes, lest Maggie forget that I was the older. Besides, I was a plain-looking child, gangly and freckled. While Maggie was acclaimed for her red-gold curls and our older sister Min commended on her baking skill—while brother Bert was admired for his gift with horses and little Willie loved for his cherubic face and merry nature, I could only be praised because I was a good girl, obedient and dependable. It was never enough for me.

"You wouldn't dare go there," Maggie said now, positively.

"I would too. I'll do it first time I know for sure he isn't around."

"Cross your heart and hope to die?"

I made the gesture and said "hope to die" with no real thought of the consequences, but within a week the almost forgotten promise loomed large and inescapable.

We were going to Ben Smythe's place with his mail, and we met Mr. Mulligan face to face in a bend of the road. We stopped and stood like startled fawns, and he stopped too, and for a long moment I looked full into his face. It was heavy-jowled and swarthy, but I saw a strange sadness there that haunted me ever after. He opened his lips as if he might speak, but then a heaviness settled on his countenance, and he closed them and brushed by us. Maggie had taken hold of my skirt and held it bunched up in her fist. Now her whisper came shrilly to my ear.

"You've got to go and knock on their door. You said 'hope to die,'" she reminded me.

I was torn between a real fear of approaching the cabin and dread of Maggie's taunts if I failed my promise. I was also afraid of the power of "hope to die."

Little Nellie was playing outside the door as we came into the Mulligans' clearing, so we stopped and called to her. She stood up, hugging a ragged little dolly against her chest and staring at us.

Then, surprisingly, Mrs. Mulligan opened the door.

"Could we have a drink of water?" Maggie asked boldly, nudging me with her elbow.

I managed to add, "And could we play with your little girl for a while?"

Mrs. Mulligan's lips curved in a faint smile.

"Come along in," she said.

The cabin was poor, even by the meager standards of that time and place. Mrs. Mulligan gave us dipperfuls of cool water from a crock near the door, and we sat on the edge of a bunk while she passed sugar cookies.

"Take two, there's more," she said proudly.

All the time we were there, she kept going to the door and looking out along the trail, and after no more than twenty minutes she said, "You'd best go now. You've a long way."

Nellie, who had been sitting in silent wonder between us, smiled and whispered good-bye as we left.

"One thing's sure, they're neither of them deef and dumb," Maggie said as we started down the trail. "And Mrs. Mulligan is kind. But he must be real mean. She only lets people in when he's away, and then she watches out the door for him."

Mother pursed her lips and a little frown flickered on her forehead when we told her of our visit.

"I don't think you should have bothered them," she said. "Leastways, don't go again, unless they call to you as you're passing."

But they did not call to us nor to anyone else, and feeling against them deepened. The gossip grew more vicious. At night, awake in my bed, I would see Mr. Mulligan's face as I had seen it that one time close at hand, and tears would well up in my eyes. They were like the tears I had shed the day Dad brought down a hawk from high above the yard, and it sprawled awkwardly in the dust and tumbled there a time before it lay still. This was the bird that had taken one of my very own chickens the day before, but I wept for it, and could not explain my tears to anyone. Afterwards, when no one was around, I took the bird, folded its wings and smoothed its feathers, and carried it into the bush. There I scooped a hollow grave. I still went sometimes and put flowers or bright leaves over the place and felt better for it. Now it seemed I should go to the Mulligans and take something bright to that dismal home. But that would be outright disobedience. If Mother should stroke my hair as she sometimes did, and say softly, "You're a good girl, Annie," would I be able to bear it?

Still, something compelled me, until finally one day I cut across the pasture, following the cattle trail to the creek, and coming out just below the Mulligan place. I had it in my mind just to stand near and see if they'd ask me in. Then I saw Mrs. Mulligan and Nellie moving slowly among the wild raspberry bushes at the edge of their clearing. Mrs. Mulligan apparently sensed my presence, for she straightened and turned to face me. For an instant her eyes held a look of alarm, but it faded as she recognized me, and she smiled. I stayed about an hour with them, picking berries and talking to Nellie, who acknowledged me shyly. After that I began to slip away for visits often, making up various excuses for my absences from home.

"I was following a whiskey-jack to see where it had its nest," I would say, or "I came upon a beaver cutting a poplar by the creek and hid and watched."

I was able to keep this up for three weeks, and saw my new friends seven or eight times. Nellie began to greet me with affection, hugging me around the knees with her bony little arms. Mrs. Mulligan smiled more, and asked me questions about my family and about school. But she gave me no clue as to why they chose to live in seclusion. Mr. Mulligan was always in the bush behind the cabin. I used the steady sound of his axe as my clue that it was safe to visit. Then one day he came in unexpectedly. I was sitting in my familiar place on the edge of the bunk with Nellie. He stood in the doorway, his great shoulders blocking it, and stared at me with an expression sober and concerned.

"It's the little Jamieson girl," said Mrs. Mulligan. "She comes to play with Nellie now and again."

Disapproval darkened Mulligan's face. He did not speak to me, but turned to his wife.

"Ellen, Ellen, how many times have I told you it's better we keep to ourselves." His tone held more of sadness than it did of anger.

Mrs. Mulligan said, "But Nellie was lonely."

He drew his lips together in a tight line, and advanced a step toward her shaking his head in exasperation.

"It's better my way, I tell you. It's better my way."

His voice rose.

Terror held me motionless. Everything I had heard about him seemed to come crowding into my brain, whirling around in a confusion of fear. Before I could move, before I could think, I heard an ugly sound and saw Mrs. Mulligan fall, headlong face down, on the rough plank floor. She lay there, and her entire body jerked and twitched with grotesque unnatural movement. There was a moan, but it came not from her, but from her husband. He had dropped to his knees beside her, and was cradling her head in his arms and talking to her in a sobbing voice.

"Ellen, Ellen forgive me. Oh God, why can't I learn patience?"

Nellie had pressed her face into the folds of my skirt and was crying softly. I could not move. Mrs. Mulligan lay quieter in a moment or so and her husband picked her up and laid her gently on the bed at the other side of the room. I caught a glimpse of his face and saw that his eyes were full of tears. Then tears coursed down my own cheeks. He took a blanket and covered his wife carefully, and then he looked at Nellie and me. For a moment his face showed only surprise; he had forgotten I was there. He came and caught me by the shoulders and his hands were hard.

"Now you will not tell what you have seen," he said. "You understand me? You will not tell anyone."

I think I must have nodded, and I think my tears softened him. He drew his hands away, touched my hair briefly and said more gently, "I am not cruel, little one. Sometimes I forget, and I shout, but I am not cruel. But there are those who are cruel. The things they say! The way they whisper, whisper. Remember now, you must not say a word."

My lips felt stiff and strange, but I managed to ask, "Is she alright?"

He nodded. "She's alright. She'll waken in a little while."

He sighed and picked up his little daughter, held her against his shoulder, and rocked her gently. I started off for home then, running headlong through the bush. When I got to the creek, I remembered my tears and stopped to wash my face, wiping it on the corner of my pinafore.

That evening after the cows were milked and the supper dishes set away, Mother went out and sat down on the low front doorstep to watch the last soft light fade from the sky. She drew up her knees and tucked her skirt around her legs, and I went and sat down beside her and leaned against her. She reached out, brushed a wayward strand of hair from my eyes and offered the old, familiar solace.

"You're a good girl, Annie."

For a long time I could not speak at all, but finally I asked the question that troubled me most.

"Mother, is it true, what old Mrs. MacIntosh says, that people who have fits have the devil inside them?"

I was shocked when Mother chuckled, but then she sobered and replied softly. "You mustn't heed what Mrs. MacIntosh says. She's a very old lady with some queer notions from times past, though she's not alone in believing them. No, fits are a sickness. You remember when Jeannie Bracken's baby had the convulsions? It's something like that, and the devil has naught to do with it, I'm sure. Such things bother you young ones sometimes!"

I was comforted, but even so I waited until time had dimmed the frightening memory of Mrs. Mulligan's twitching body before I went to visit Nellie again. It was a drizzly day, chill with fall, when I finally slipped away. More than anything I wanted them all to know that I had kept their secret. I was hoping they would smile and say I was a good girl. I was in the midst of my favorite daydream, in which I saw myself grown beautiful and famous, when I realized I was in a new clearing. It was dotted with stumps and piles of slash. A corner of Mulligan's land extended across the trail here and he had begun to take timber from it. I stopped to look around, and heard a low call from the far side.

At first I thought it was some kind of animal, but it came again, and I knew it for a man's voice. Then I saw there was a huge tamarack tree freshly down, and something stirring its branches. I went over as quickly as I could, picking my way over the rough ground, and found Mr. Mulligan lying in the tangle with the great trunk of the tree across his thighs. His face was beaded with sweat and his eyes were dulled with pain, but he smiled a little.

"You were coming to play with Nellie after all," he said, as though this were the most important thing.

I nodded and we looked intently at each other. There was nothing I could do for him alone, and we both knew it, but the need of secrecy still bore heavily on us, so when we talked about getting help, we did it apologetically.

"I'll have to get my father," I said.

"It's the only thing to do," he agreed. "I think one leg is broken. I'll have to be taken to town."

"Father will take you," I said. I wondered if Mr. Mulligan understood that along with his secret I'd had one of my own to keep.

"It will be a great shock to Mrs. Mulligan," I whispered and waited.

"She should not be upset—it will . . ." His voice trailed away.

I took my handkerchief from my pocket and knelt down and wiped his face with it. It was what I always did for little Will when he came to me with a scraped knee or cut.

"My mother will look after her," I promised. "She saved Jeannie Bracken's baby that had the convulsions. And she won't talk of it, believe me, Mr. Mulligan."

His eyes lighted a little, and he reached his hand to my sleeve.

"You're . . ." he began and I waited for the familiar "a good girl," but these were not the words he spoke.

"You're a brave girl," he said. "You'll be a fine, beautiful woman some day."

I got up. My skirt clung wetly to my shaking knees and I shivered in the cool, misty air. I had been deceitful and disobedient and now it would be known, but it came to me that I had been no more wicked than the hawk that soared above the yard, then swooped to take my chicken, for I too, had done only what I thought I must.

"I'll not be long, and it's going to be alright, Mr. Mulligan," I said, and somehow my voice sounded strangely like my mother's.

Then I tore off through the clearing like a colt newly freed from its first wearing of a saddle.

Perky and energetic Beatrice Fines has been a free-lance writer about 20 years, with stories and articles in Canadian, American and Scottish magazines and newspapers. She does public relations work for the Health Sciences Centre of Winnipeg and teaches creative writing in continuation education classes.

"He knew he must find his way
through that cave, or hole, or tunnel,
and out the other side."

Through the Tunnel

BY DORIS LESSING

**A boy's compulsion to prove himself . . .
dramatic, handsomely crafted and upbeat!**

GOING to the shore on the first morning of the vacation, the young English boy stopped at a turning of the path and looked down at a wild and rocky bay, and then over to the crowded beach he knew so well from other years. His mother walked on in front of him, carrying a bright striped bag in one hand. Her other arm, swinging loose, was very white in the sun. The boy watched that white naked arm, and turned his eyes, which had a frown behind them, towards the bay and back again to his mother. When she felt he was not with her, she swung around. "Oh, there you are, Jerry!" she said. She looked impatient, then smiled. "Why, darling, would you rather not come with me? Would you rather—" She frowned, conscientiously worrying over what amusements he might secretly be longing for, which she had been too busy or too careless to imagine. He was very familiar with that anxious, apologetic smile. Contrition sent him running after her. And yet, as he ran, he looked back over his shoulder at the wild bay; and all morning, as he played on the safe beach, he was thinking of it.

Next morning, when it was time for the routine of swimming and sunbathing, his mother said, "Are you tired of the usual beach, Jerry? Would you like to go somewhere else?"

"Oh, no!" he said quickly, smiling at her out of that unfailing impulse of contrition—a sort of chivalry. Yet, walking down the path with her, he blurted out, "I'd like to go and have a look at those rocks down there."

She gave the idea her attention. It was a wild-looking place, and there was no one there; but she said, "Of course, Jerry. When you've had enough, come to the big beach. Or just go straight back to the villa, if you like." She walked away, that bare arm, now slightly reddened from yesterday's sun, swinging. And he almost ran after her again, feeling it unbearable that she should go by herself, but he did not.

She was thinking, Of course he's old enough to be safe without me. Have I been keeping him too close? He mustn't feel he ought to be with me. I must be careful.

He was an only child, eleven years old. She was a widow. She was determined to be neither possessive nor lacking in devotion. She went worrying off to her beach.

As for Jerry, once he saw that his mother had gained her beach, he began the steep descent to the bay. From where he was, high up among red-brown rocks, it was a scoop of moving blueish green fringed with white. As he went lower, he saw that it spread among small promontories and inlets of rough, sharp rock, and the crisping, lapping surface showed stains of purple and darker blue. Finally, as he ran sliding and scraping down the last few yards, he saw an edge of white surf and the shallow, luminous movement of water over white sand, and, beyond that, a solid, heavy blue.

He ran straight into the water and began swimming. He was a good swimmer. He went out fast over the gleaming sand, over a middle region where rocks lay like discolored monsters under the surface, and then he was in the real sea—a warm sea where irregular cold currents from the deep water shocked his limbs.

When he was so far out that he could look back not only on the little bay but past the promontory that was between it and the big beach, he floated on the buoyant surface and looked for his mother. There she was, a speck of yellow under an umbrella that looked like a slice of orange peel. He swam back to shore, relieved at being sure she was there, but all at once very lonely.

On the edge of a small cape that marked the side of the bay away from the promontory was a loose scatter of rocks. Above them, some boys were stripping off their clothes. They came running, naked, down to the rocks. The English boy swam towards them, but kept his distance at a stone's throw. They were of that coast; all of them were burned smooth dark brown and speaking a language he did not understand. To be with them, of them, was a craving that filled his whole body. He swam a little closer; they turned and watched him with narrowed, alert dark eyes. Then one smiled and waved. It was enough. In a minute, he had swum in and was on the rocks beside them, smiling with a desperate, nervous supplication. They shouted cheerful greetings at him, and then, as he preserved his nervous, uncomprehending smile, they understood that he was a foreigner strayed from his own beach, and they proceeded to forget him. But he was happy. He was with them.

They began diving again and again from a high point into a well of blue sea between rough, pointed rocks. After they had dived and come up, they swam around, hauled themselves up, and waited their turn to dive again. They were big boys—men, to Jerry. He dived, and they watched him; and when he swam around to take his place, they made way for him. He felt he was accepted and he dived again, carefully, proud of himself.

Soon the biggest of the boys poised himself, shot down into the water, and did not come up. The others stood about, watching. Jerry, after waiting for the sleek brown head to appear, let out a yell of warning; they looked at him idly and turned their eyes back towards the water. After a long time, the boy came up on the other side of a big dark rock, letting the air out of his lungs in a sputtering gasp and a shout of triumph. Immediately the rest of them dived in. One moment, the morning seemed full of chattering boys; the next, the air and the surface of the water were empty. But through the heavy blue, dark shapes could be seen moving and groping.

Jerry dived, shot past the school of underwater swimmers, saw a black wall of rock looming at him, touched it, and bobbed up at once to the surface, where the wall was a low barrier he could see across. There was no one visible; under him, in the water, the dim shapes of the swimmers had disappeared. Then one, and then another of the boys came up on the far side of the barrier of rock, and he understood that they had swum through some gap or hole in it. He plunged down again. He could see nothing through the stinging salt water but the blank rock. When he came up the boys were all on the diving rock, preparing to attempt the feat again. And now, in a panic of failure, he yelled up, in English, "Look at me! Look!" and he began splashing and kicking in the water like a foolish dog.

They looked down gravely, frowning. He knew the frown. At moments of failure, when he clowned to claim his mother's attention, it was with just this grave, embarrassed inspection that she rewarded him. Through his hot shame, feeling the pleading grin on his face like a scar that he could never remove, he looked up at the group of big brown boys on the rock and shouted *"Bonjour! Merci! Au revoir! Monsieur, monsieur!"* while he hooked his fingers round his ears and waggled them.

Water surged into his mouth; he choked, sank, came up. The rock, lately weighted with boys, seemed to rear up out of the water as their weight was removed. They were flying down past him now, into the water; the air was full of falling bodies. Then the rock was empty in the hot sunlight. He counted one, two, three . . .

At fifty, he was terrified. They must all be drowning beneath him, in the watery caves of the rock! At a hundred, he stared around him at the empty hillside, wondering if he should yell for help. He counted faster, faster, to hurry them up, to bring them to the surface quickly, to drown them quickly—anything rather than the terror of counting on and on into the blue emptiness of the morning. And then at a hundred and sixty, the water beyond the rock was full of boys blowing like brown whales. They swam back to the shore without a look at him.

He climbed back to the diving rock and sat down, feeling the hot roughness of it under his thighs. The boys were gathering up their bits of clothing and running off along the shore to another promontory. They were leaving to get away from him. He cried openly, fists in his eyes. There was no one to see him, and he cried himself out.

It seemed to him that a long time had passed, and he swam out to where he could see his mother. Yes, she was still there, a yellow spot under an orange umbrella. He swam back to the big rock, climbed up, and dived into the blue pool among the fanged and angry boulders. Down he went, until he touched the wall of rock again. But the salt was so painful in his eyes that he could not see.

He came to the surface, swam to shore and went back to the villa to wait for his mother. Soon she walked slowly up the path, swinging her striped bag, the flushed, naked arm dangling beside her. "I want some swimming goggles," he panted, defiant and beseeching.

She gave him a patient, inquisitive look as she said casually, "Well, of course, darling."

But now, now, now! He must have them this minute, and no other time. He nagged and pestered until she went with him to a shop. As soon as she had bought the goggles, he grabbed them from her hand as if she were going to claim them for herself, and was off, running down the steep path to the bay.

Jerry swam out to the big barrier rock, adjusted the goggles and dived. The impact of the water broke the rubber-enclosed vacuum, and the goggles came loose. He understood that he must swim down to the base of the rock from the surface of the water. He fixed the goggles tight and firm, filled his lungs, and floated, face down, on the water. Now he could see. It was as if he had eyes of a different kind—fish eyes that showed everything clear and delicate and wavering in the bright water.

Under him, six or seven feet down, was a floor of perfectly clean, shining white sand, rippled firm and hard by the tides. Two grayish shapes steered there, like long, rounded pieces of wood or slate. They were fish. He saw them nose towards each other, poise motionless, make a dart forward, swerve off, and come around again. It was like a water dance. A few inches above them the water sparkled as if sequins were dropping through it. Fish again—myriads of minute fish, the length of his fingernail—were drifting through the water, and in a moment he could feel the innumerable tiny touches of them against his limbs. It was like swimming in flaked silver. The great rock the big boys had swum through rose sheer out of the white sand—black, tufted lightly with greenish weed. He could see no gap in it. He swam down to its base.

Again and again he rose, took a big chestful of air, and went down. Again and again he groped over the surface of the rock, feeling it, almost hugging it in the desperate need to find the entrance. And then, once, while he was clinging to the black wall, his knees came up and he shot his feet out forward and they met no obstacle. He had found the hole.

He gained the surface, clambered about the stones that littered the barrier rock until he found a big one, and, with this in his arms, let himself down over the side of the rock. He dropped, with the weight, straight to the sandy floor. Clinging tight to the anchor of stone, he lay on his side and looked in under the dark shelf at the place where his feet had gone. He could see the hole. It was an irregular, dark gap; but he could not see deep into it. He let go of his anchor, clung with his hands to the edges of the hole, and tried to push himself in.

He got his head in, found his shoulders jammed, moved them in sidewise, and was inside as far as his waist. He could see nothing ahead. Something soft and clammy touched his mouth; he saw a dark frond moving against the grayish rock, and panic filled him. He thought of octopuses, of clinging weed. He pushed himself out backward and caught a glimpse, as he retreated, of a harmless tentacle of seaweed drifting in the mouth of the tunnel. But it was enough. He reached the sunlight, swam to shore, and lay on the diving rock. He looked down into the blue well of water. He knew he must find his way through that cave, or hole, or tunnel, and out the other side.

First, he thought, he must learn to control his breathing. He let himself down into the water with another big stone in his arms, so that he could lie effortlessly on the bottom of the sea. He counted. One, two, three. He counted steadily. He could hear the movement of blood in his chest. Fifty-one, fifty-two. . . . His chest was hurting. He let go of the rock and went up into the air. He saw that the sun was low. He rushed to the villa and found his mother at her supper. She said only "Did you enjoy yourself?" and he said "Yes."

All night the boy dreamed of the water-filled cave in the rock, and as soon as breakfast was over he went to the bay.

That night, his nose bled badly. For hours he had been underwater, learning to hold his breath, and now he felt weak and dizzy. His mother said, "I shouldn't overdo things, darling, if I were you."

That day and the next, Jerry exercised his lungs as if everything, the whole of his life, all that he would become, depended upon it. Again his nose bled at night, and his mother insisted on his coming with her the next day. It was a torment to him to waste a day of his careful self-training, but he stayed with her on that other beach, which now seemed a place for small children, a place where his mother might lie safe in the sun. It was not his beach.

He did not ask for permission, on the following day, to go to his beach. He went, before his mother could consider the complicated rights and wrongs of the matter. A day's rest, he discovered, had improved his count by ten. The big boys had made the passage while he counted a hundred and sixty. He had been counting fast, in his fright. Probably now, if he tried, he could get through that long tunnel, but he was not going to try yet. A curious, most unchildlike persistence, a controlled impatience, made him wait. In the meantime, he lay underwater on the white sand, littered now by stones he had brought down from the upper air, and studied the entrance to the tunnel. He knew every jut and corner of it, as far as it was possible to see. It was as if he already felt its sharpness about his shoulders.

He sat by the clock in the villa, when his mother was not near, and checked his time. He was incredulous and then proud to find he could hold his breath without strain for two minutes. The words "two minutes," authorized by the clock, brought close the adventure that was so necessary to him.

In another four days, his mother said casually one morning, they must go home. On the day before they left, he would do it. He would do it if it killed him, he said defiantly to himself. But two days before they were to leave—a day of triumph when he increased his count by fifteen—his nose bled so badly that he turned dizzy and had to lie limply over the big rock like a bit of seaweed, watching the thick red blood flow on to the rock and trickle slowly down to the sea. He was frightened. Supposing he turned dizzy in the tunnel? Supposing he died there, trapped? Supposing—his head went around, in the hot sun, and he almost gave up. He thought he would return to the house and lie down, and next summer, perhaps, when he had another year's growth in him—*then* he would go through the hole.

But even after he had made the decision, or thought he had, he found himself sitting up on the rock and looking down into the water; and he knew that now, this moment, when his nose had only just stopped bleeding, when his head was still sore and throbbing—this was the moment when he would try. If he did not do it now, he never would. He was trembling with fear that he would not go; and he was trembling with horror at the long, long tunnel under the rock, under the sea. Even in the open sunlight, the barrier rock seemed very wide and very heavy, tons of rock pressed down on where he would go. If he died there, he would lie until one day—perhaps not before next year—those big boys would swim into it and find it blocked.

He put on his goggles, fitted them tight, tested the vacuum. His hands were shaking. Then he chose the biggest stone he could carry and slipped over the edge of the rock until half of him was in the cool enclosing water and half in the hot sun. He looked up once at the empty sky, filled his lungs once, twice, and then sank fast to the bottom with the stone. He let it go and began to count. He took the edges of the hole in his hands and drew himself into it, wriggling his shoulders in sidewise as he remembered he must, kicking himself along with his feet.

Soon he was clear inside. He was in a small rock-bound hole filled with yellowish-gray water. The water was pushing him up against the roof. The roof was sharp and pained his back. He pulled himself along with his hands—fast, fast—and used his legs as levers. His head knocked against something; a sharp pain dizzied him. Fifty, fifty-one, fifty-two . . . He was without light, and the water seemed to press upon him with the weight of rock. Seventy-one, seventy-two . . . There was no strain on his lungs. He felt like an inflated balloon, his lungs were so light and easy, but his head was pulsing.

He was being continually pressed against the sharp roof, which felt slimy as well as sharp. Again he thought of octopuses, and wondered if the tunnel might be filled with weed that could tangle him. He gave himself a panicky, convulsive kick forward, ducked his head, and swam. His feet and hands moved freely, as if in open water. The hole must have widened out. He thought he must be swimming fast, and he was frightened of banging his head if the tunnel narrowed.

A hundred, a hundred and one . . . The water paled. Victory filled him. His lungs were beginning to hurt. A few more strokes and he would be out. He was counting wildly; he said a hundred and fifteen, and then, a long time later, a hundred and fifteen again. The water was a clear jewel-green all around him. Then he saw, above his head, a crack running up through the rock. Sunlight was falling through it, showing the clean, dark rock of the tunnel, a single mussel shell, and darkness ahead.

He was at the end of what he could do. He looked up at the crack as if it were filled with air and not water, as if he could put his mouth to it to draw in air. A hundred and fifteen, he heard himself say inside his head—but he had said that long ago. He must go on into the blackness ahead, or he would drown. His head was swelling, his lungs cracking. A hundred and fifteen, a hundred and fifteen pounded through his head, and he feebly clutched at rocks in the dark, pulling himself forward leaving the brief space of sunlit water behind. He felt he was dying. He was no longer quite conscious. He struggled on in the darkness between lapses into unconsciousness. An immense, swelling pain filled his head, and then the darkness cracked with an explosion of green light. His hands, groping forward, met nothing; and his feet, kicking back, propelled him out into the open sea.

He drifted to the surface, his face turned up to the air. He was gasping like a fish. He felt he would sink now and drown; he could not swim the few feet back to the rock. Then he was clutching it and pulling himself up onto it. He lay face down, gasping. He could see nothing but a red-veined, clotted dark. His eyes must have burst, he thought; they were full of blood. He tore off his goggles and a gout of blood went into the sea. His nose was bleeding, and the blood had filled the goggles.

He scooped up handfuls of water from the cool, salty sea, to splash on his face, and did not know whether it was blood or salt water he tasted. After a time, his heart quieted, his eyes cleared, and he sat up. He could see the local boys diving and playing half a mile away. He did not want them. He wanted nothing but to get back home and lie down.

In a short while, Jerry swam to shore and climbed slowly up the path to the villa. He flung himself on his bed and slept, waking at the sound of feet on the path outside. His mother was coming back. He rushed to the bathroom, thinking she must not see his face with bloodstains, or tearstains, on it. He came out of the bathroom and met her as she walked into the villa, smiling, her eyes lighting up.

"Have a nice morning?" she asked, laying her hand on his warm brown shoulder a moment.

"Oh, yes, thank you," he said.

"You look a bit pale." And then, sharp and anxious, "How did you bang your head?"

"Oh, just banged it," he told her.

She looked at him closely. He was strained; his eyes were glazed-looking. She was worried. And then she said to herself, Oh, don't fuss! Nothing can happen. He can swim like a fish.

They sat down to lunch together.

"Mummy," he said, "I can stay underwater for two minutes—three minutes, at least." It came bursting out of him.

"Can you, darling?" she said. "Well, I shouldn't overdo it. I don't think you ought to swim any more today."

She was ready for a battle of wills, but he gave in at once. It was no longer of the least importance to go to the bay.

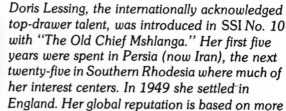

Doris Lessing, the internationally acknowledged top-drawer talent, was introduced in SSI No. 10 with "The Old Chief Mshlanga." Her first five years were spent in Persia (now Iran), the next twenty-five in Southern Rhodesia where much of her interest centers. In 1949 she settled in England. Her global reputation is based on more than twenty books—short stories, novels, reportage, plays and poems. The Golden Notebook is probably her best known work.

"He reacted instinctively and lashed out
with a left and a right to the head."

Sparring Partners

BY IAN SEARLE

**Humorous and poignant . . .
two men of the cloth lose their veneer.**

"FISH again!" said Father Lenotre, sitting down wearily.

"The Sisters do their best, Father; it isn't easy, you know," Father Barthier said.

Lenotre did not answer, trying hard not to be irritated by this smug little priest who was always so charitable. For three years he had shared his life and work with this man who remained steadfastly cheerful in the face of death, disease, privations, the heat, mosquitoes and all the other oppressive facts of life at this isolated mission. It would be a further four years before his mandatory seven-year term of service expired and the cross would be lifted from his shoulders.

Lenotre's lined face, gaunt with years of hardship and yellowed by quinine, looked briefly even sadder than usual.

"Come now, Father," said Barthier, "it's not that bad; indeed, it's really very good fish. Sister Marie is a remarkable cook. We're very fortunate."

He smiled encouragingly, and Lenotre looked at him in disbelief, seeing a round pink face that retained its color in spite of the fierce tropical sun. Why, he wondered, must he continue to jolly me along like a sick child who needs to be humored? Why can he not for one instant talk to me as an intelligent adult? Why can't he simply say I'm bad-tempered and should control myself?

But Lenotre said nothing, just ate a little food, pushed the plate away and lit his pipe.

"We're running very low on medical supplies," he said at length. "I hope the ship arrives soon."

"I'm sure the Bishop is doing his best," said Barthier.

"I'm sure, too. I only wish he could do better. We have almost no drugs left."

"We must have faith, Father."

"We must have quinine, too."

"It will come."

"Yes, of course it will—eventually. But it's already three weeks late. The first week in November, we were told. Now it's December. Christmas will be on us soon."

"Astonishing how quickly time passes, isn't it?" said Barthier. "The last time the ship called we were preparing for Holy Week."

Barthier finished his meal with a couple of mangoes. Then Sister Marie scurried in with the coffee, put it on the table and left without saying a word or raising her eyes. Lenotre poured two cups and drank his quickly. Gratefully, he left the table and went to his room. Lying half-naked under the mosquito-net he sweated gently. His book remained unopened beside him. He heard Barthier's bed creak and the grunts and puffing as he arranged himself on the other side of the thin bamboo wall. After a few minutes the heavy breathing gave way to loud snores. Lenotre heaved a deep sigh of resignation and opened his book.

Lenotre loved the solitude, the chance to reflect, to meditate on his life as a priest, to pray. If only it were not for the snoring, the two-hour silence after lunch would be perfect. A faint breeze stirred the mosquito-net. The square hole that was the window showed palm-fronds and a blue sky beyond. The children from the little school had been sent to lie down for an hour before they began their daily gardening. Cicadas sawed away, making their shrill noise that passed unnoticed until it stopped.

Lenotre began to pray. Forgive me, Lord, for my uncharitable thoughts. I really do try to remember all the good things about Barthier. I know he means well and it is I who am at fault. He has a simple faith, Lord, while I am so often troubled with doubts and so easily led into cynicism. It is not his fault he irritates me, and he always seems so cheerful because he believes we all need cheering up. There are times when I feel very old and tired, when my dearest wish is to be alone, as I am now. It is then Barthier annoys me the most because he will not leave me alone; he always reminds me of my duty; he always expects me to put on a cheerful face. He makes me feel inadequate, Lord, and that is a heavy cross to lay on any man. I know this is your way of testing me. Help me pass the test; help me keep my patience; help me to be humble. Now I'm being sorry for myself, too. Lord, I'm a weakling. Help me conquer my weakness; help me to think of others, especially of Barthier, and to help him. We have never been close, in all the time we have spent together here. He must have a strength that I lack. I shall try to admire it more.

Lenotre sat up, mopped his forehead and picked up his book. He could not concentrate and, after a minute or two, put the book down again, got off his bed and padded, barefoot, to the shower. The water was warm but refreshing, and yet five minutes later, as he sat on the veranda in clean clothes, he felt as hot as before. There was no escape from the humidity.

He looked out across the sea and indulged in his favorite disciplinary exercise. He forced himself to look at the view and seek again the pleasure it had first given him, the pleasure any newcomer would find.

In front of the house rough grass swept down to the brow of the hill with its fringe of ragged wild shrubs. On either side bushes framed the picture. The tall bare gray trunks of kapok trees rose sharply above shorter, green crowns. At the foot of the hill coconut palms swayed slightly, their fronds glittering. The lagoon was a mixture of deep blues and vivid greens where the coral grew relentlessly upwards and through the surface of the water. The surf broke in a white line over an almost continuous barrier reef. Then there was nothing but sea, blue and unbroken. For a moment Lenotre felt again the splendor of the scene which he saw every day.

Suddenly he stiffened and stared hard at the horizon. Returning to his room he fetched his old binoculars and focused them on a small black mark in the distance.

"Father Barthier! Father!" he called.

His companion appeared on the veranda a few minutes later. His round face was still bloated with sleep, like that of a small child. "What is it?" he asked, running his fingers through his dishevelled hair.

"The ship. I think it's coming at last. Take a look."

Rubbing the sleep from his eyes Barthier took the glasses and looked out to sea. "Yes," he said. "I said we should have faith."

Lenotre suppressed his irritation. "She'll just make it by nightfall. We'd better warn the Sisters. The Bishop will want a good meal—and we'd better get the children ready, too."

There was much to do. It was a point of honor to have the Mission spick and span when the Bishop made his call. The children were recalled from the gardens to tidy the schoolrooms and dormitories. The two priests set about tidying their own house, while the Sisters worked with some of the children in the little church, filling it with flowers and changing the altar cloth, before they set to work in the kitchen, preparing a meal for their visitor.

This was an occasion in every sense: not only were visits rare—once or twice a year—but they were welcome in many ways. They allowed the Fathers to make confession and provided the opportunity to obtain advice and guidance on the thousand problems which had arisen. For the children there was a chance to show their skills to an important visitor. A visit also provided an excellent reason for having a traditional feast.

At length the preparations were complete: the Mission was neat and tidy and every doorway was fringed with palm-fronds, the ends of which had been stripped to the centre rib and scarlet hibiscus flowers spiked on the tips. Banana leaves were spread in a broad pathway across the lawn and little parcels of food, wrapped in yet more leaves, lay thickly on the improvised table-cloth which was liberally decorated with hibiscus and frangipani blooms. The children were scrubbed and garlanded, their thick, curly hair almost hidden under leaves and flowers. The four Europeans wore spotless robes.

The whole community lined the beach as the schooner tacked to approach the entrance to the lagoon. She was painted black and stained by the sea; her sails were brown. She was business-like, but to the watchers on shore she was sheer beauty. At length she hove to, her sails were dropped, and the anchor splashed into the shallow water. The Bishop was rowed ashore in a dinghy manned by four oarsmen.

He greeted the Fathers and the Sisters in French, then, turning to the children, spoke briefly to them in their own language, saying how pleased he was to see them all again.

He turned back to Father Lenotre. "Would you ask the children to stay here and help unload the ship while we go on up to the Mission? I'm afraid we must unload tonight and sail again at first light. But I have a surprise for you."

"A surprise, my lord?"

"Yes, indeed. We have six tea-chests full of gifts from the people of my old parish of Saint Antoine. They made a collection of all kinds of things and sent them to us to give to the Missions—especially with the children in mind."

At the house the Bishop took a shower before accepting a drink of cold lime juice.

"It is lovely here," he said, staring out from the veranda as the brief dusk fell. The sky was a blazing mixture of orange and gold; the white line of breakers seemed alive. Lamps on the schooner illuminated it like a chiaroscuro painting. The children, carrying boxes up from the beach, sang as they worked.

Lenotre looked at the Bishop. "I am sorry you can't stay longer."

The Bishop turned towards him with a smile. "And I'm sorry there is so little time to sit and talk. You have a difficult and lonely task to do. The two of you must try to give each other support as well as set an example to your flock. It isn't easy. We will make the most of the few hours we have. First I shall hear your confessions and those of the Sisters; then we shall say a mass."

Lenotre and Barthier stood on the beach in the early morning and waved a last farewell as the ship sailed away. "He's a good man," observed Barthier.

Lenotre could not think of an appropriate answer. He remembered what had passed in the privacy of the confessional and was grateful at least that the Bishop understood his personal trial.

"Yes," he answered at last, "I'm always sorry to see him go. He brings a strange comfort with him."

"Comfort," repeated Barthier in his most irritating manner. "That's a peculiar word to use. He is a godly man, of course. Is that what you mean?"

"Yes," said Lenotre. "Shall we go back?"

"Let's give the children a treat," said Barthier. "They can help us unpack the tea-chests. They'll enjoy that."

They set out the chests in a line in front of the house. "Come on, Benedict," said Barthier to a boy standing near the front of the crowd of curious children. "You open the first box."

The boy levered off the lid and began to remove the contents.

"And what have we here?" asked Barthier, in his jolliest voice. Reaching into the chest he pulled out two pairs of boxing-gloves. Lenotre could not believe his eyes.

A small boy asked, "What are they, Father?"

"Boxing-gloves, my boy," said Barthier. He untied them and pulled one on. "See?"

The children looked at his gloved hand, not understanding.

"They're for boxing; it's a sport," explained the priest. "Look." He put on the other glove, raised his clenched fists in a parody of a prizefighter and indulged in a little shadow-boxing.

The children were too respectful to laugh, but they were puzzled at the priest's antics.

"I don't think they understand you," Lenotre observed drily.

"No, I don't think they do." Barthier was puffing slightly from his exertions. "Father Lenotre and I will show you," he said to the children. "You see, it needs two men. They both wear gloves like these." He tossed the second pair to Lenotre. "And they box in a square space—like the veranda there. Come on, Father." He clambered up the steps and Lenotre followed him.

"Do you think this is a good idea?" asked Lenotre.

"Of course! Is there any better way to explain? Put the gloves on."

Lenotre hesitated, then did so while Barthier tried to explain what boxing was all about.

"You see?" he said. "The two men shake hands to show they are not real enemies, then they begin to box—to hit each other. Come on, Father!" He threw a playful punch at Lenotre.

Lenotre shrugged. He had become involved in this and did not want to make Barthier look even more foolish in front of the children. He would have to play along with him. He began to spar, flicking lefts at his opponent, who still laughed his jolly laugh and punched playfully back.

Lenotre, tiring of this half-hearted game, stopped moving and dropped his gloves just as Barthier swung a wild right. The blow caught Lenotre square on the left check-bone and, for an instant, he saw red. He reacted instinctively and lashed out with a left and a right to the head. The left caught Barthier high up on the temple. A trickle of blood ran down his face. The smile disappeared and on Barthier's face Lenotre was surprised to see an undisguised dislike which matched his own. He wanted to hit that face, to vent the years of frustration on this stupid, pretentious, condescending priest. He did so, lashing out in earnest, forgetful of the surroundings, of the crowd of children watching open-mouthed. Barthier retaliated with less skill but with equal fury, swinging wildly at the taller man, the gaunt, cynical companion who treated him with an almost aristocratic contempt. Fists whirled and smacked, and the two men staggered and gasped on the veranda. Lenotre suddenly unleashed an enormous left hook which knocked Barthier off his feet, hurling him headlong off the veranda to land in a crumpled senseless heap on the grass.

Lenotre looked down at him, gulping in air and sweating profusely. The children were now terrified, having become aware that the fight was serious. The priest pulled off the gloves and stepped down from the veranda. With the help of several children he managed to carry Barthier into the house where they placed him on the sofa. Lenotre told the children to go. They went, quietly and with fearful glances at the unconscious figure on the couch.

There was a large red swelling on Barthier's right cheek-bone. Gently Lenotre pulled the boxing-gloves from his companion's hands and fetched a damp face-cloth with which he bathed Barthier's face. A bewildering confusion of thoughts ran through his head. When he hit Barthier he had experienced, momentarily, great satisfaction, but now he felt only shame. Looking down at the still figure he was shocked to find that it was like looking at a stranger—the round face, normally full of sincere cheerfulness, was now relaxed into an expression of sadness, almost of suffering. For the first time in three years Lenotre felt a real pity and an affinity with the little man.

Barthier stirred and opened his eyes, He looked up at Lenotre and frowned. Gathering himself together, he put a hand up to his face.

"Father," said Lenotre, "forgive me. I didn't mean. . . ."

"It's all right," said Barthier. He tried to smile but winced suddenly at the pain. "There's no real harm done."

"Barthier," insisted Lenotre, "I think you should know—it wasn't an accident. I wanted to hurt you. I'm ashamed."

"There's no need," said Barthier. "I know you were in earnest. But then, so was I. For a moment we both forgot ourselves. I hope we're both sensible enough to dismiss it from our minds."

"But I've hurt you!"

"Not seriously. I admit I feel a little shaky, but I expect I'll recover."

"Let me bring some wine."

"That would be nice."

The two men sipped the wine in silence, then Barthier said quietly, "I had this coming, you know. Perhaps it's as well it happened."

"What do you mean?"

"I think you know what I mean." Barthier did not meet his eyes.

"We've lived and worked together now for three years in this place; in all that time I've been a great trial to you, I know."

"A trial?"

"Please, Father, let's be honest with each other. When we joined the Order we both accepted that we had no control over our own lives, our place of work, our companions. Personal preferences are not allowed in our work. We promise obedience. It is not always easy. It is probably harder for you you than for me."

Lenotre did not reply. He agreed, although it was a painful truth.

"You see, I'm not a very clever man and I accept it. I just about managed to scrape through all the examinations at the seminary. My only regret is that I can do so little for you because you are intelligent."

"Even if this were true," said Lenotre, trying to comfort him, "there are gifts more important than intelligence—charity, patience, cheerfulness, unselfishness."

"Perhaps. Perhaps. But for someone like you, Father, I am about the worst companion. I put on a cheerful face every morning. I pretend to be the eternal optimist, to keep everyone cheerful. It's my way of atoning, you see, for my insufficiency. I know you suffer loneliness and have the burden of responsibility for the Mission, of caring and planning for the school and the sick. You are so much cleverer than I. You always see the problems first and always find the answers."

"Oh, come now, Barthier," said Lenotre, beginning to feel uncomfortable. "You do your fair share, you know. And you are cheerful. You do a lot of good, putting heart into everybody when the heat gets us down, or when the rains spoil the gardens, or when we're feeling dispirited with fever."

Barthier shook his head. "It's only an act, Father. It's all I can do. The trouble is, you know that, and, I regret to say, I resent your knowing it."

"I don't understand."

"After three years," said Barthier, "I still find you remote. Our backgrounds are so different; your parents were bourgeois, comfortably off, used to mixing with intelligent, well-educated people.

I come of peasant stock. I still find it hard to talk to people, so I act a part. I'm the jolly, fat, friendly little priest; you're the clever, sharp and decisive man, destined perhaps for a high post in the Church.''

''You mean I'm cynical and sarcastic.''

''That too, at times, when foolish people exasperate you.''

''Father,'' said Lenotre, ''why are you telling me all this? Wouldn't it be better left unsaid?''

''I'm saying it because I need your forgiveness as much as you need mine.''

''My forgiveness?'' Lenotre was startled.

''I wanted to knock you down when we started boxing. Inevitably you knocked me out, just as you will always better me at anything. Still, I really wanted to hurt you.''

Lenotre got up and walked towards the veranda. Far out to sea the schooner, a tiny black speck, was about to slide over the horizon. The children had disappeared, leaving a litter of clothing and empty boxes on the grass. Lenotre felt tired and drained, aware of the isolation and the burdens of the work. ''I'm sorry,'' he said, with his back to the room. ''You must find me terribly difficult to work with.''

''Not to work with, Father; your work is first class. It's just that we are such an ill-matched pair—me, an inarticulate fool, and you, a competent leader.''

''Pride,'' said Lenotre with emphasis, ''that's all it is, dammit. I'm too proud. I keep myself to myself, talk only to the Bishop and to God. I get annoyed with you when you are simply doing what you think is best, instead of treating you with respect as an equal. You are right, Father, to be angry with me.''

''No, you can't justify anger like that.''

Lenotre turned back to his companion. ''I think you can,'' he said, ''because you have taught me a valuable lesson today.''

''What's that?''

''We're both human. I might be a better boxer than you, Father, but I'm certainly not a better Christian. Let's have another glass of this excellent wine, then you can tell me where I can find a hammer and a nail.''

"What do you want them for?"

"You'll see."

Ceremoniously, Lenotre hammered a nail into the wall. Then he picked up the two pairs of boxing-gloves and, tying them together, hung them on the nail. Finally he poured two glasses of wine. "A toast," he announced, "to the day we discovered we are both human."

They raised their glasses and drank.

Lenotre sat down opposite Barthier and smiled at him over his glass. Barthier lifted his own glass in salute. His pink, round face, still swollen, was completely serious.

Trained as a teacher at Oxford University, Ian Searle taught for six years in England before accepting the post of Education Officer in the Solomon Islands. Four years later he returned to teaching in England. At present he manages a newsagent's and writes in his spare time.

"Spread out along the bottom of the pool
there lay a thin, coarse layer: my old rust."

Imaginary Monologue

BY GÜNTER KUNERT

Sophisticated fantasy . . . a whimsical spellbinder.

I'M not denying anything. It all comes under the statute of limitations anyway. I admit that I've snatched a few forest rangers since 1730. They smelled terrible and usually tasted like tobacco, hartshorn and unwashed loden, and that should be reckoned enough punishment for my appetite. But I haven't touched another forest ranger for more than a hundred years now. Looking back at it, I get sick thinking of those full-bearded, green shapes, crazy about trees, with ears overgrown with thick, bushy hair, listening raptly to nerve-wracking bird noises. I've got much too delicate a sensibility to be able to stand this unceasing screeching, cuckooing, trilling, whistling, warbling. But these forest rangers, ever since they've existed—or, rather, ever since I've known them—stand spellbound, as if hearing the grandest music of Lizt or Toselli while enveloped by the morning mists, with a first ray of sunshine penetrating the moldering branches. Meanwhile my hand stretches out softly from the center of the lake where I'm at home and I grab them by their green necks and put them out of their romantic misery. I don't deny it. But even so it's not prosecutable under the statute of limitations. And there were never any witnesses in the vicinity. Potential circumstantial evidence, like remains of clothing, shoulder bones or indigestible shoe leather, has long since dissolved in the quagmire. And there's no net fine enough to trap an infusorian which, by reacting to birdsong, might reveal what transformations of matter it has undergone.

Forest rangers are boring. If you crack their skulls, you find nothing but hunting junk. Virtually nothing new about the great, vast world on dryland. It's a long time since I've talked to a human being.

A few days ago something was swimming around down here, a queer creature I'd never seen before: instead of feet it swam with flippers, there were two round bulges protruding from its back, its face consisted practically of only one big flat eye, two curved tubes hung down from its mouth, and little air bubbles were always coming out of it! At first I thought it was a kind of strayed seacow without an udder until I addressed it and it stopped dead in terror and then in a mad dash climbed to the surface. Then I recognized it: it was a human being. I reached out after him with my gigantic iron hand, happened to hit up against a rapidly rotating screw jutting out of the stern of a boat and would have had my fingers torn off if I weren't made of iron. As it was, it only scratched off a little of the rust that I'm covered with all over. There was a time when I used to clean off the rust myself, once in a while, in order to take pleasure in my smooth iron rump but I soon outgrew that youthful vanity. The rust returned after a little while anyway, and so I let it grow until it formed a thick rough bark around my body—the color of dying embers. I still remember what heat is: fire, I saw it for the first and simultaneously last time shortly after I was born. There's no mystery whatever about my origins.

My mother was a simple miller's daughter but my father was of the very highest ancestry. He wished to preserve his incognito at the time and actually so should I now too if I weren't compelled by my respect for science and my liking for Dr. Mullberger to disclose unreservedly everything that concerns me.

When in the summer of 1719 this miller's daughter went out to pick blueberries and was filling her little basket, a noble gentleman rode down that lonely path, a gentleman for whom basket miller's daughter and jumping off his horse was a single act. Before the (to date chaste) maiden was even able to stand up—drowsy as she was from the sticky heat of the forest and stunned by the intense sunlight—it was already too late. With impunity the horseman had ravished her from behind. And as she meanwhile piteously beseeched her ravisher for his name so that her child would at least know that much about its father, a voice behind her bellowed rudely: "Theirs is not to reason why, theirs is but to do and die!"

At that moment she realized whom she had to thank for her subsequent fate: King Frederick William I who had been riding from village to village on this sweaty day in July in the year of Our Lord 1719 checking up on his subjects—unrecognized, so he thought. Not much later it became obvious that her excursion into the forest had borne fruit—whose consistency, however, was something of a mystery. For the weight of the life growing in her made it impossible for the miller's daughter after only three months to stay on her feet. She spent six months in bed before giving birth to twins: there were two of us, you see. Me, Ironjack, and him, Nickelpeter. About him, more later. When the midwife pulled me out into the world and lifted me up, she was so surprised at my weight that she dropped me out of fright. I heard her scream that the brat had fallen on her foot: Ow, she was bleeding, the instep of her foot must be broken . . . "Miller's daughter, miller's daughter, what is it that you've given birth to?" And my dear embarrassed mother replied that the noble sire had looked quite normal insofar as he'd been visible during conception: a big, fat man in a blue jerkin. His broad shoes with real silver buckles were what was most vivid in her memory. Meanwhile the midwife was moaning: "Lord, help us, the kids are made of metal! You're a witch, Miller's daughter, you've been carrying on with the devil . . ." And off she rushed straight to the Tax Office to register a formal accusation. Shortly thereafter legal proceedings were instituted which concluded with the death sentence: the said miller's daughter, together with her two homunculi, conceived by her of Beelzebub as she herself had admitted on the rack, were to be sewn up in a tight bag and dropped into the biggest pond far removed from the city limits. And whereas she had sought to inculpate the King in this satanic intercourse, she was in addition to be deprived of her civil rights by reason of lése majesté.

And so we were immersed: the three of us. Our mother drowned. We, her metallic sons, of course didn't. Any sort of pulmonary breathing turned out to be superfluous. We only felt a voracious appetite every now and then. Then we would devour fish and since that time these waters are uninhabited. We grew. With our powerful claws we grabbed the wild animals that came to the water's edge to drink. Nickelpeter was the first to grab a forest ranger but we gobbled him up together. We divided everything up between us. In the evenings, as it got murkier and murkier under the water, we would ponder and speculate about our own materiality, without being able to arrive at any explanation. Only later was it analyzed for me scientifically, after my brother had already emigrated to England. This is how it happened.

One whole burning summer long the water level of our pond dropped lower and lower—it must have been 1760—and we could hardly stand up without risk of being seen. So we spent most of the time resting and daydreaming in the mud. A farmer, seized by the absurd hope of catching a barbel or a stickleback, rocked back and forth above us in the square shadow of his dinghy. We pulled him down to us and found out from the trembling fellow that a war had been going on for seven years already. The fields weren't being worked and people were going hungry. Pressed for more, he stammered: The war's against Austria. Frederick William I's son is personally leading our troops.

Our half-brother! What's he made of: iron or copper or what? We wanted to know and got for an answer: I can't understand your question, sirs. But all objects made of metal are being collected and melted down for cannon and shot.

While chewing pensively on the meagre bones of the farmer, we considered how odd it was that our half-brother, a certain Fritz, was made of real flesh and blood. Nickelpeter, a rather timorous character, was afraid of being melted down as soon as the water dropped further and we would be discovered. He wanted to forestall the violent breakdown of his personality into militant spherical masses and made up his mind to escape that very night through one of the brooks running out of our pond. He seemed to have disappeared without a trace, seemed to have vanished unnoticed God knows where, until I found out from an Englishman—who though tough on the outside, was quite tender on the inside—that my brother was now in Loch Ness. He's often seen there but he isn't caught because the British S.P.C.A. has officially declared him a "Royal Monster" and hence in need of preservation. Our mutual physio-chemical origins which I hadn't understood because of my poor scientific training were only clarified in the 20th century however.

My rustbark kept on growing, my iron face was covered with lichen and algae which I removed once a year by means of a scraper. I carried out this process hidden among the rushes and bent over the water, which I used as a mirror, scraping off the annoying green muck from my cheeks. I had hardly shoved my head out into the air this time, blinking in the bright sunlight, snorting and dripping water out of my ears and mouth, with my knuckles pressed into the sandy beach, when I suddenly heard somebody yelling:

"Hold it, you over there! You're getting my fishing lines all fouled up, you damned lout!"

I shouted over to him that the pond belonged to me, that I was the terrible Ironjack and that I didn't allow anybody to mock me. But the guy in the boat answered: "We Germans fear God alone, and nothing else in the world. I'm Professor Emeritus Andreas Schulmann and fish wherever the law allows!"

I: "The only reason there's no law against it here is because there aren't any fish anymore. What time do we have now? I mean: what year is it?"

He: " It's 1912. It seems to me you must be a foreigner. From somewhere along the eastern shore of the Baltic, with some Mongoloid blood as the shape of your skull seems to suggest."

I explained to him that I was born in the area, but he shook his tangled white mane: "Nonsense. I'm a geneticist. I know you much more thoroughly than you know yourself."

"What's a geneticist?" I asked, and he explained it to me, twirling his pince-nez on its black band. He struck me as really the only possible person to explain my incomprehensible genesis. He listened breathlessly to my confession, soon tears rose into his eyes and he muttered excitedly: "A Hohenzollern, a real Hohenzollern! The striking forehead, the shield of world-embracing designs, mindful of the grandeur of the Empire, the stern nose, the chin— yes, Your Royal Highness has convinced me! Your Royal Highness, I am entirely at your service!"

I: "Why is it that I'm made of iron?"

He: "A remarkable but by no means mystical process. As far as is known, His Majesty Frederick William I possessed an iron character which probably served as a genetic catalyst. At that time the King was undergoing mercury treatment for his gout—being medicated with quicksilver—prescribed for him by a medical science still in its infancy. His character, acting as a catalyst, must have structurally transformed the quicksilver circulating in his body, and in his testicles as well, into iron or, respectively, nickel. An astonishing and most royal result. The spermatozoa, now of the same chemical composition as metal, but alive, couldn't produce anything other than metallic beings, an iron man: You, my Prince!"

I was so dumbfounded that I neglected to internalize this remarkable scholar, something that would have aided the development of my personality enormously. Instead, I simply gaped while he seized his oars, bade me a respectful farewell and in a flash was swallowed up by the reeds—rustling mockingly—instead of by me. He was the first to get away undigested. Thus this second of confusion and lack of decisiveness proved to be the cardinal error of my life—as it later turned out.

I must have dozed off for a while after settling back comfortably once again in the mud, pondering the mystery (now unveiled) of my earthly existence, an existence which I could only enjoy in a submerged state because on land my weight impedes all of my movements. I slept for at most a few little years. I woke up suddenly and with a jolt. Thought I'd heard distant thunder. Rolled over grudgingly on my other side. Then another shock wave jolted me wide awake. Inky slime whirled up into my eyes, the all too perceptible crashing noises of explosions broke out close by—not above but below the surface—and forced me to rise up. It was raining up there. On the shore stood men in black uniforms. One of them yelled: "There he is, Oberscharfuehrer!" And the man so designated put this funnel to his lips and addressed me:

"Hey, you listen to me, Comrade Ironjack! I'm Oberscharfuehrer Schulmann! My father told me about your pristine steely German might. Now that Final Victory is nearly at hand we've got to make use of all our reserves of strength. Your steely strength too. The country needs fellows like you. If you refuse to do your duty we've got even better things than hand grenades. We've got underwater demolition bombs. Not an eye dry after you use those! We've managed to take care of the defeatists so far, get it? So, OK, tomorrow morning a crane will come and pick you up. A toothbrush and a change of underwear will be enough. Sieg Heil!"

The dark shapes slipped away under the trees. Billions of little drops of water made them invisible. As the forest stood silent in the rain before me like a murky three-dimensional tapestry, I almost doubted that anybody had been there. But my environment was still utterly convulsed and obscured by the explosions. Underwater detonating bombs, eh? I thought about whether Schulmann, Jr. wasn't actually right to ask for my help. Oughtn't I to be grateful to my country for the forest rangers? And after all the country couldn't be held responsible for their unappetizing nasty and felt-like taste. Didn't I have my countrymen to thank for those robust girls who went out looking for mushrooms and who practically melted in your mouth? Being German means: Being easy to digest! In spite of my iron constitution: underwater detonating bombs, eh? I decided to be a loyal subject of my fatherland, which I knew only in a fluid state. They would undoubtedly send me into action along the coast in order to sink ships or something like that. One blow from my fist against the hull and the cruiser would go to the bottom. I was sure of getting a medal. I already saw myself with the Order of the Black Eagle or with the Golden Fleece, soldered onto my freshly de-rusted chest, towering out of the waves of the German Atlantic, a living monument to victory, girded by the raging surf, a Germanic Poseidon, the source and fount of a new myth of the sea-conquering tribe of Teutons.

As if charged with an ambivalent tension almost like electricity, I sleeplessly waited for dawn. It came. But no Schulmann Jr., no vehicle to transport me away. This was my greatest disappointment of the last few decades and the reason why I withdrew resentfully into the relaxing mud, there to reflect upon the geopolitical role which inexplicable circumstances had prevented me from playing. Shouldn't I just utterly renounce all earthly pursuits? Nevermore to emerge to the surface? Simply rust away sadly, to be discovered in future millennia, an unsightly lump of scrap iron on which once the fate of Prussia hinged? Serves them right: if they don't want me, they can and should lick my . . . even if they get blood-poisoning in their tongue in the process.

I stuck to my decision for a long time, until something came diving down to me, a queer shape that might credibly have been an udderless seacow till I spoke to it and it took off in horror for the surface. Then I noticed: it was a human being. I made a grab for him. Went up after him. A boat sped away leaving a wake of loud screams behind. An uneasy presentiment filtered through me. The loudmouths in the speedboat would doubtlessly broadcast their encounter with me through the whole world. My peace had departed. Handgrenades, eh? Underwater detonating bombs, what? Who knows what kind of monstrosities they'd invented.

I waited in the deepest spot in the lake for what I had imagined would come. I didn't have to wait long until the hull of a ship floated past above me, large and oval shaped, a rubber ellipse. As I was peering up there, they lowered a can on a string. The cap was off and an amber-colored fluid oozed in delicate clouds out of the container. Then my memory stopped functioning. Suddenly it was night.

When it grew light again, I was lying at the bottom of a tiled pool in lukewarm water, with the taste of perfumed soap in my mouth, free of the algae and mussels that had inhabited my back and derrière, and enveloped by a net of steel wire. Over the edge of the pool, a bald head, with glasses, beard, and looking like a seadog, peered down at me: You, Dr. Mullberger, and you said: "Good morning, Ironjack. How do you feel?" And I answered: "Where am I? How did I get here?" Then you again:

"You are in a scientific research institute, my good fellow. I'd almost given up hope of finding you. For twenty years now we've had in our safe the report of an SS-Oberscharfuehrer about an encounter with you. The report was never sent off because he died in action. A friend of the dead officer, a metallurgist, took the report and after the end of the war delivered it to his company and they then passed it on to us for evaluation. Can you imagine, Ironjack, the number of ponds, puddles and bodies of water I've searched through? Because the dead officer had forgotten to make a note of the place. When I heard the news last evening of your surfacing in Devil's Pond, there was no time to be wasted. At four in the morning we reconnoitred the bottom with a mine-detector and—zammo! We got you. Anaesthetic in the water, wire cable round your neck, towed to shore, loaded on a truck and zowee: to the Institute. On the way back hordes of reporters and curious onlookers met us. We managed to steal a march on them. You can congratulate yourself. Now you can kiss rust goodbye."

Every morning Dr. Mullberger appeared at the pool. Out of various other little bottles he dropped various compounds into the water. Was it a solution of hydrochloric acid? A corrosion preventative? In any event I woke up one morning completely clean and bright as a boy. Spread out along the bottom of the pool there lay a thin, coarse layer: my old rust. Proudly I examined my limbs and they reflected so much light in the water that Dr. Mullberger had to approach me wearing sunglasses. Although I asked him every morning why he'd dragged me out of my home in the pond, he always shook his head and smiled: "Just hold on Ironjack. The future's already begun. We need you badly, old friend. How do you feel this morning?"

"Very fine, thanks, Doctor. Quite young. As if I hadn't been born in 1720, but only twenty years ago."

The next morning a girl's face leaned down over my shining

iron nakedness.

As a child of the 18th century that made me feel an unsuspected embarrassment. I tried to hide myself, she tittered. She pushed herself out further over the edge of the pool in order to empty a little tube of milky viscous stuff and in the process showed a pair of naked shoulders. Still a little further. I lowered my eyes because her sweet little bulges weren't covered by anything either. I believe a reddish glint spread over my gleaming exterior. On the next day I had the courage to raise my eyes. And after a week I had gotten used to seeing her completely nude. Hence I wasn't dumbfounded when one morning she appeared in company with other girls, just as unpeeled as she was. The first was blonde, the other brunette. The third had freckles all over, the fourth was suntanned. With the eighth, I didn't notice details anymore, and when there were about twenty of them camping around my pool, I could hardly manage to keep them apart. They didn't rouse my appetite in the least. Even when they took away the wire netting over my head and I could easily have reached up with my gigantic hand and pulled down a breakfast for myself. Incomprehensible: I'd lost all of my savagery. Maybe they'd mixed some hunger depressant in with the water. Or perhaps the lukewarm water just made me drowsy. I didn't even make a grab for them when they splashed around shamelessly on the surface. Not even when they dived. They got quite close, touched me with their little soft paws and in doing so set something in my breast moving like a steamhammer. They fluttered around me like mermaids, Nereids, nixies, sirens, nymphs—or whatever other name you want to give to temptation—until I yielded to their incessant attack. Nine months later Dr. Mullberger comes up to my pool, nods, smiles says: "Congratulations, Ironjack, you've become a father today. Precisely twenty times. Twelve daughters, eight sons."

I: "Thanks, Doctor, I'm awfully embarrassed about it."

"Nonsense, Ironjack. That's what you're here for. Oh my yes, I'd completely forgotten to inform you of the reason for your stay in our Institute. So now you know it."

I answered him that I'd confessed my life history to him in good faith, even the business with the forest rangers (though falling under the statute of limitations), while he . . . he kept quiet about his intentions of misusing me. Until now. Until he now delivered this lecture:

"We're in need of people with constitutions like yours. Through people like you, Ironjack, we're getting in reach of that long sought-for ideal of an absolutely frictionless historical process. The present species of homo sapiens—that lacrimose, eternally hungry, eternally unsatisfied creature torn by conflicting emotions—will be gradually replaced by a species sprung from your seed. Only an iron humanity is ordained to rule the universe, and I, Dr. Horst Mullberger, will be its prophet!"

He makes a gesture with his right hand, hides his left hand behind his back: a clumsy movement, and I perceive that he's hiding a little bottle from me: full of the same amber-colored substance which I remember only too well. Asked about it, he replies curtly: "You've done your duty. You can go back now to your pond."

Suddenly it's as if a yellow fog is seething down through the water and no matter how far I retreat into the opposite corner—still it reaches me. As I gradually lose consciousness I see how kind Dr. Mullberger keeps on dumping bottle after bottle into the water and, dropping off, I wonder what's the point of the overdose . . .

Epilog: Advertisement in the Classified Section of the *Daily Mail:* Circa two tons of highest quality iron (the faulty cast of a statue) for sale considerably below scrap iron price: Dr. H. Mullberger, Institute for Macrobiology.

Born 1929 in Berlin, Günter Kunert was excluded from military service during World War II on "racial" grounds. He studied at the Academy of Applied Arts in Berlin-Weissensee and attracted the attention of Johannes R. Becher, with his satirical poems and stories. He also writes for radio and motion pictures. Peter E. and Evelyn S. Firchow translated the story; they are husband and wife, teach on the college level and translate skillfully.

"The secret is to know their tender spots,
their pet vanities . . ."

Domino

BY SUJATHA BALA SUBRAMANIAN

Women were his pawns . . . almost always.

"INDIRA," he called me. He looked at me as if I were a person
instead of just a piece of furniture. It is always Indu baby or Indu
sweetie at home. They don't realize how one can grow and grow
inside all by one's self and never show it. Sometimes I look at the
girls in class and think I might belong to another planet. There are
so many things I can never discuss with them. Would they understand if I simply said, "He is so handsome." They would only
giggle and gaze at me slyly. I really had no business being there
that night, but Mother said, "It's time Indu met a few people and
we are only going to the Anand's, it's just the family." I decided to
wear my orange for it usually shows off my dark skin to advan-
tage. It could have been another evening of "Hello. Are you
Anand's niece? What are you studying?" If I had said zoo-keepng,
they would have certainly gone on with "How interesting, and
what will you be later on?" with half an ear cocked towards the

person on the left. But he looked at me silently for a moment and said, "What lovely hair you have, Indira." I flushed and didn't know what to say. "Here," he said, handing me a glass of tomato juice, "why don't we sit down for a while?" After a short pause I blurted out, "I liked *The Strange Noon* very much." "It is one of my good books," he replied gravely. "What did you think of *A Fool's Mountain*?" "Ohh! I haven't read that yet," I answered. He settled himself more comfortably in the chair and said, "Tell me, do you write?" I had never told anyone about them before, but within ten minutes I was promising to show him my poems. I was sorry yet glad in a way when he rose saying, "Bring them to me tomorrow will you?" All eyes appeared to be staring at us. Afterwards, it was good to watch him from across the room. How easily he mixed with the others. Even that teacher, Uncle Anand's neighbor, he was being kind to her though she was so old and dowdy. I went over the poems mentally, thinking I'd have to write them all out neatly again, wondering which lines he would like. The gray at his temples, how distinguished it looked. His eyes met mine over the heads of the people and he smiled.

You sit at the mirror and wonder. The past doesn't unroll and the future is far away. It is now that counts. Just once, oh! God! you pray, just once, let me kindle that special look, just once before it is too late. Always, there is the impending doom of time. The sands are running short. Every time you add that extra dab of perfume and carefully go over the already darkened eyelid; it has to be today, the special day. But eyes everywhere are glazed and dull and you keep searching each face, avoiding the avid, predatory hands that press yours moistly. Every summer that could be yours leaves only another strand of gray which is hidden artfully behind the ears. Then you think of him, you've only seen him once, and say to yourself it can't be and it must be and you don't know whether to hate yourself for everything; the summer with no stacks of exercise books to sweat over; the summer with its hordes of new faces thrust upon the carefully cultivated crust of peace. "Drop in Thursday evening," says Mala, "we are having a friend staying with us for the season and I would like you to meet him."

Premnath the novelist, tall, graying handsomely at the temples, world-weary and most charming. He has seen them all before and you, little mousy you are the most interesting person he has met! Oh! You could see through it all when you have been on the search a whole lifetime. You can see how he sums you up at first glance; widow, young enough to want a man's attention. Sometimes you wonder yourself what it is you want, turn sour when you intercept a smug smile on a woman's face. This man, he is subtle. There are no crude, insincere compliments to make you draw into your shell. He talks like a man of the world with just that spark of interest in the right places, till you soon begin to feel you are somebody, you are a wonderfully different person than the rest. You go along with the game, crying inside; just this once, couldn't it be true, just this once? Can you say when it is that you steel your heart against the life and smile into his eyes? At the doorstep, he places the wrap around your shoulders as Mala says, "Now, don't forget, we are off at nine. It is a stiff climb, so have a good night's rest."

They are all the same, young or old. A little flattery, a little attention and they are at your feet begging for it. The secret is to know their tender spots, their pet vanities and before you realize it you will have them falling all over you. Oh! It needs a lot of working out all right. You need the same perfection of technique as for the book you have been working on. But both ways you can't say I haven't done well. There is such a thing as a public image and it does help sales if you have that extra charm. The pretty ones, they know they are all right, but it's those in the background that thaw out most perfectly. You work on them gently or they shy away. Many a time, I've laid bets with myself, this one should be eating out of my hand before dessert is served or that—she's not the type at all. You'd be surprised how they all like hearing about Uma. My wife, I say, she loves this shade of blue and already some kind of barrier seems to go down. It never does to go in for that old my-wife-doesn't-understand-me routine and bachelors seem to have that little disadvantage when it comes to scoring with them. Now, this evening I have already marked the field. There are two of them, but what a contrast. There's this young slip of a girl, she should flower out beautifully with correct handling, but it'll be strictly on the level. I'm no heel. The other, she's different, could be something there for a pleasant summer. The picnic in the morning would be the right time to shorten Sumitra to Sumi; perhaps a quiet talk in a corner, but compliments are definitely out. This one I have to watch my step with. She should be quite a few years younger than I but I keep forgetting that I am forty-five if a day! The red shirt should do nicely for tomorrow, with a scarf maybe. She could go into one of my books, there is something latent here that might be worth getting on paper.

There were quite a lot of poems to choose from and I could take only a few to him the first time. It was not very hard to select, I had my own favorites. But I threw in a couple which I felt were not too good. How could I guess what he would like? He read through them silently at first and my heart hammered suffocatingly. Suppose he said they were terrible! Then he read them again more slowly. "A horde of dancing suns . . .," he read aloud. "That is a good line and also the next," he remarked with a smile. "You can write sensitively but I feel your endings could be tidier. For instance . . ." I only half-heard what he said after that. My eyes were down, my knees shook and I could only look at his strong brown hands as they held my poems. "Have you any more?" he asked me and I nodded dumbly. "Well, let me have a look at them and I could get you to go over the bad patches again. You could make something really worthwhile out of them if you tried." As he handed over the papers to me he took my hand in his. "What beautiful fingers, smooth and delicate!" But in a moment everything was spoilt, for this school teacher came over to speak to him. I went home without even thanking him.

I saw him the next Friday when Aunt Mala had arranged another picnic for all of us. Mother was about to let me out of it but I wangled and hinted and got asked too. It was a glorious day. He spoke to me about a lot of things and for once I felt I was a person in my own right without fearing that I was going to put my foot in it everytime I opened my mouth. He was so strong and yet I felt he could be tender when I looked into his eyes. I should have realized that it wouldn't last. Oh! Why did she have to come and spoil it all. I saw them walking in the dark that night, so close to each other, her head almost on his shoulder. They turned in at the gate and stopped by the door for a minute. Then he took her in his arms and kissed her, crushing her to him with all his strength. She reached up and twined her arms behind his neck abandonedly. The door opened and they vanished into the blackness beyond. I ran. I ran all the way home crying to myself "How hateful, beastly, horrible—." I shut myself in the bathroom and retched for a long time, sobbing and beating my hands on the cold basin. Later, I washed my face and went to my room. The first thing I did was to open my desk and take out my file of poems. In five seconds I had reduced them all to a heap of fragments which I angrily swept into the waste-paper basket.

Who are you to draw the line between light and shade? It is uniformly gray here and if your eyes are blind enough the sun will rise and dance for you today. For one thing you give thanks, never once does he call you darling, never, when that hot word could burn up the fragile scaffolding you are ascending on. You watch as it builds up piece by piece, black on white, mix and match. You watch as he twists that young girl around his finger, watch with amusement and pity as he deliberates over the scrupulously neat lines on the foolscap. There's just that mixture of careful attention, judicious praise and spotting of weak points that holds her enthrall-ed, a slave for life. Soon he turns to you and remarks with a casual shrug "These youngsters have to be humored, you know. Now, where were we—?" His eyes flash a conspiratorial look. A fortnight's too long to know him, you've had him tagged the first minute. You play the game his way, match his five with a two, thinking you can shake yourself out of this dream anytime you chose. And don't forget that unless you dream you will never see the sun. So, who wants to wake up anyway? The secret is to live the dream with your eyes wide open. But the moment his arms close around you, you know you will never awaken from this for it is no dream. In some dim recess of your mind you can hear yourself whispering Arun, Arun, but that was twenty years ago. Now is all that matters. There was no past and there will not be a future after the death of this moment. Now there can be nowhere to hide yourself so you come out on the stage as you are. You can't say when the lie disappears from between the two of you, when the game ends and reality begins. One thing is clear, common people like you can't live the truth forever. No two persons can face each other for long without layers of grease-paint. Thank God, there are no complications. He doesn't say what shall we do. You can almost see it coming when he decides to go back to his wife soon. What else is there to do? This surfeit should last you all your life. You go to the station to see him off for the last time and again you are relieved that he has no common-place cliché to offer you as a parting gift. The train steams out and soon you are the only one left on the platform.

I tell myself I am going to enjoy this holiday. There is a peculiar thrill when I am half-way down a book, a sense of contentment. There is no going back, you want to write the last word in a hurry and get it out of you. That is what I feel now. About the girl, there is no trouble, I have a tailor-made role; one that I have played before. She is too young to learn that one lives a thousand lives before a page can be written. Sumitra, she appears to be ripe for the occasion. My judgment of her seems to be correct and I can plan each move confidently. It is quite an experience, almost like living a chapter in a book when the chips fall where you want them to. But as soon as I touch her I think "Oh! God! What have I started?" Only for a moment I realize that I should have a mask, but now, suddenly, there is no line between what I seem and what I am. No woman should give so much of herself. She makes me a begger, I who have always been the dispenser of alms. The lot of them, all the tender little speeches in my repertoire remain unsaid. I cease to be the director even when I whisper "Sumi" once or twice involuntarily. A nameless, faceless being is what I am, all my props knocked down from under my feet. At Anand's I explain to Mala that my wife wants me back home urgently and wave one of

Uma's old letters around. The next train is at five in the evening. It has to be this way, both of us know it and there is no need for words. The alternative is beyond contemplation. So little is said and so much understood and I don't even wonder it is so. Somewhere along the way the masquerade has ended and I have faced a moment of truth. Our hands meet for the last time and I get into the train. This is when I might have said "I love you," but somehow, I am glad I didn't and I am sure she is too.

Born 1932 in Madras, Sujatha Bala Subramanian has been writing since she was nineteen. Her stories appear in periodicals and journals in India and England. She has twice won the Roscoe Award for the best short story in U.K. and Commonwealth. The author travels widely, is married to an aeronautical engineer and has two daughters.

"But you were lazy. You preferred contemplation. It was easier, it didn't raise a sweat . . ."

The Decline and Fall of Our Local Mosque

BY A.A. NAVIS

In listing deadly weapons, don't overlook the power of a story.

A few years ago, your bus to the town I was born in would have dropped you at the market. If you had walked a mile down the road and taken the fifth lane to the right, you would have found an old mosque, with a fishpond and four purification pools in front of it. In the yard to the left of the mosque, you would have met an old man who sat there piously. Zealously he sat for years, as though he was the caretaker. People used to call him Grandfather.

He received nothing for looking after the mosque. He lived on the alms he received from those attending Friday service. Once every six months, he was given a quarter of the fish taken from the pond. Once a year, he was given part of the offering for the poor. He wasn't the caretaker. He was a knife-sharpener. He was very good at his trade. People used to ask him to help them because he never asked for payment. The women gave him chili sauce when he sharpened their scissors and knives. The men gave him cigarettes and, sometimes, money. But usually he received "Thank you" and a smile.

He doesn't live there anymore. He is dead. No one looks after the mosque anymore. Children play in it. Women pull boards from the walls and floor when they run out of firewood at night. Your impression now would be one of decayed sanctity. The decay increases with each passing day, as the children run wild and the women keep their fires alight. The world is more ignorant and careless than it was.

I want to tell you how this decline first started. It is, of course, a true story.

Once I came to ask Grandfather to do something for me. He was usually pleased to see me, because I used to give him money, but this time he looked very depressed. He sat right in the corner of the yard, with his knees tucked tightly under his chin and his arms around his legs. He stared mournfully ahead as though some fever was running through his brain. Scattered around his feet were his tools of trade: an old condensed milk tin filled with coconut oil, a whetstone, a long piece of shoe leather, and an old cut-throat razor. I had never seen him looking so miserable before. He had never refused to return my greeting. I sat down next to him and took up the razor. "Whose is this, Grandfather?" I asked.

"Ajo Sidi's"

"Ajo Sidi's?"

He said nothing. Ajo Sidi was a garrulous old man. I hadn't seen him for a long time; he could hold people all day with his strange talk, but seldom did. He worked too hard. He gained greatest satisfaction when people in the town were labelled with names of characters in his stories. Once there were elections. He told us about a frog whose only ambition in life was to be a king. We called one of the politicians "the frog prince."

I wondered if the old man had been subject to Ajo Sidi's interminable nonsense. Was that what had made him so miserable? I was curious. "What did he talk to you about?" I asked.

"Who?"

"Ajo Sidi."

"Oh. That bastard," he replied wearily.

"Why?"

"I've sharpened his razor for him. I hope he cuts his throat with it."

"You're angry with him?"

"Angry? I would be if I was younger, but I'm not. We old people aren't hot-heads. I haven't lost my temper for years. I'd be afraid of jeopardizing my faith. I might ruin it completely. I've tried to be good, to dedicate myself to God and do all He commands. I've tried to surrender myself to him completely. He loves those who are patient and submissive."

I wanted to know the whole story, exactly how Ajo Sidi had made the old man so angry. So I asked again: "What did he talk about, Grandfather?"

He didn't answer. Perhaps he was too upset. But I kept at him and he finally told me. "You know me, don't you? I was here when you were a boy. When I was a boy. You know the sort of things I've done. Have I ever done anything I shouldn't have? Anything God would be angry at me for doing?"

I said nothing. I knew that once he started, it was difficult to stop him. I let him answer his own question.

"You know how long I've been here. I've never once thought of getting married and having a family. Never. I've never wanted to be rich or have my own house. My whole life—body and soul— has been for God, blessing and glory be His. I've never hurt anyone. I don't even like killing the flies. But now he says that I'm damned. Fit for hell. Do you think God will be angry with me? Will He curse me for serving Him? I've never worried about tomorrow. God exists and He is merciful and compassionate to those who love Him. I get up before dawn and beat the drum so everyone can wake up and pray. I pray all the time, day and night, morning and afternoon. His name is always on my lips. I read His book. If something good happens, I say: 'Praise be to Allah.' If something upsets me: 'God forgive me.' If something unusual happens, I say: 'God's will be done.' I've never done anything wrong. And now he tells me I'm damned . . ."

I waited a few minutes and then asked: "Is that what he said?"

"Not exactly. But that was what he meant."

He cried. I felt sorry for him. Silently I swore at Ajo Sidi. Yet I wanted to know more. Finally he started again.

"Once upon a time—that's how Ajo Sidi put it—God sat in the hereafter examining the dead one by one. He had appointed certain angels to sit with Him, and in their hands they had lists of all the good and bad things the people had done. There was a war on earth and He had quite a lot of people to get through. One of the newcomers was called Haji Saleh 'the pious man who completed the pilgrimage to Mecca.' Haji Saleh smiled all the time. He wouldn't have any trouble getting into Heaven. He put his hands on his hips and puffed out his chest. He looked up cheerfully with his head thrown back. His lips curled mockingly as others flew down to hell. He waved to them as if to say 'bye-bye.' The queue was never ending, as it moved forwards to God, others joined at the rear. God examined every man thoroughly.

"Finally it was Haji Saleh's turn. He bowed to God and smiled proudly. Then God asked him His first question: "And you?"

"I'm Saleh. I've been to Mecca, Lord."

"I didn't ask what your name was. I don't need names. Names are of no use here . . ."

"Yes, my Lord."

"What did you do on earth?"

"I prayed to You all the time, Lord . . ."

"What else did you do?"

"Nothing you forbade, Lord. I never did evil, even though the devil filled the whole earth with temptation . . ."

"What else?"

"Nothing, Lord. I prayed and recited Your holy name continually. Even when I was sick, Your name never left my lips, thanks to Your great mercy. I prayed always that sinful mankind would be won over by Your loving kindness . . ."

"What else?"

Haji Saleh was silent. He had told God all that he had done. But he knew that God wasn't asking just for the sake of asking. Yet he had told Him everything he could think of, and was unable to think of anything he had omitted. Suddenly he felt the warmth of the fires of hell licking at his body. Each tear he cried evaporated.

"What else?" God insisted.

"I have told you everything, O Lord God, most merciful and compassionate, righteous and omniscient—" Haji Saleh was worried. He tried humility and flattery, hoping that God would feel more kindly disposed towards him and not ask him the wrong questions.

But God asked him once more: "Nothing else?"

"Hm, hm, aah—I don't know, O Lord—I always read Your holy book . . ."

"Nothing else at all?"

"I've told You all I know, Lord. But if I have forgotten anything, I praise your omniscience . . ."

"So you only did the things you told Me?"

"Yes, Lord."

"Enter—" and a beautiful angel led Haji Saleh down to Hell by the ear. Haji Saleh couldn't understand it. He didn't know what else God had wanted him to say and he couldn't believe that He had made a mistake.

Surprisingly, many of his friends were in Hell too, suffering the agonies of the damned. This was even more confusing, for they were all at least as pious as he was. Some of them had been to Mecca fourteen times and could even claim to be descended from the holy prophet Muhammad himself. They were as confused as he was.

"What has God done?" Haji Saleh asked them. "We served Him faithfully and did all He commanded. We spent our whole lives in obedience to Him and now He sends us to Hell—"

"You're right. That's exactly what we think too. Just look at us, all fellow-countrymen and none of us less faithful than the others."

"It's not fair!"

"No, it's not!" they repeated.

"We have to see the records. An audit to make sure He hasn't put us here by mistake."

"True. True. True," they all shouted in agreement.

"What if He refuses to admit that He's made a mistake?" a shrill voice called from the crowd.

"We'll draw up a petition and hold a demonstration," said Haji Saleh.

"What sort of petition?" a former radical politician asked.

"We can work that out later," replied Haji Saleh. "Let's demonstrate first."

"That gets the best results," someone else cut in.

"Right. No doubt about it. True," they shouted.

So they walked up to God, making an awful row.

God took off His old-fashioned, gold-rimmed spectacles and put them on the table beside Him. "What do you want?"

Haji Saleh, leader and chief spokesman, intoned their complaint in a hesitant, beautifully rhythmic voice: "O Almighty God, we come before You as faithful servants who have worshipped You all our lives. Your name was ever on our lips. We praised Your greatness and Your righteousness and Your ninety-seven other attributes as well. We learnt Your holy book by heart and never read it. But, O Lord Omnipotent, after You called us to Your side, You thrust us down to Hell. We have no wish to see anything unpleasant happen and so, in the name of those who love You, I insist that You re-examine the judgment You bestowed upon us, so that we can enter the Heaven You promised us in Your holy book—"

"You are all fellow-countrymen?"

"Your faithful servants are all from Indonesia, O Lord—"

"A very fertile country, is it not?"

"Yes, Lord."

"A very rich country, full of minerals, oil and other natural resources?"

"Indeed it is, Lord, thanks be to You. We are all Indonesians," they all said at once. Their faces shone with delight. They were convinced that God had indeed made a mistake in sending them to Hell.

"A country of rich vegetation?"

"Yes. No doubt about it. True. That's where we come from."

"A country rife with poverty?"

"Yes. Yes. Yes. That's the one."

"A country owned by foreign interests?"

"Yes Lord. Terrible oppression. Very bad."

"Who take what you grow back to their own countries?"

"It's true, Lord. We don't get a penny back. They are cruel—"

"A country in such chaos that you fight amongst yourselves while this goes on?"

"Yes, Lord. We never cared about material possessions. Our only goal was to praise and worship You—"

"You didn't mind being poor?"

"No, Lord. We preferred it."

"You didn't mind that your descendants would be poor too?"

"No, Lord. They may be poor but they know the *Koran* by heart—"

"But it means nothing to them, just as it means nothing to you?"

"Oh no, Lord!"

"Then why did you remain in poverty, making no provision for those to come? You let others steal your property, while you fought amongst yourselves, you deceived and oppressed each other. I gave you a rich country. But you were lazy. You preferred contemplation. It was easier, it didn't raise a sweat, and required no exertion. I told you to work and pray. You only prayed. You thought that I wanted praise, that I was intoxicated by your worship to Me, so you did nothing but praise Me and glorify My holy name. You must go back to Hell! Angels—drive them back! Put them in the lowest pits!"

They were pale and too terrified to say anything. At last they understood the sort of life they should have led.

Haji Saleh still did not know whether his life had been well or badly spent. Because he did not dare ask God, he asked the avenging angel instead: "Did I do wrong worshipping God?"

"No. You did wrong in spending too much time on the cultivation of your soul. You prayed because you were afraid of going to Hell, but you forgot your fellow Muslims and your family. You were put in the world to live as part of a community, but you were too selfish."

That was Ajo Sidi's story, the story that had so greatly distressed the old man.

I thought of going for a walk the next morning. My wife asked me if I was going to the funeral.

"Who's dead?" I asked in surprise.

"Grandfather."

"The old man?"

"They found him at dawn. It was horrible. He cut his throat wide open with a razor."

"My God! All because of Ajo Sidi!" I exclaimed as I quickly hurried out.

I went to Ajo Sidi's house. Only his wife was at home. I asked her where he was.

"He's gone," she replied.

"Does he know that Grandfather is dead?"

"He does. He told me to buy seven lengths of winding cloth."

"Where—" I was appalled by Ajo Sidi's total irresponsibility. "And now where is he?"

"Gone to work."

"He has?" I asked emptily.

"Yes. He's gone to work."

A.A. Navis was born in Padang, Sumatra, in 1924. He has published several volumes of short stories.

"The poor kid is a half-orphan already.
Why make him a full one?"

Disgrace

BY GIDEON TELPAZ

A young person's private agony during political turbulence.

THE quarry was always close by on the other side of the road. You couldn't see it from Uncle Yiftach's workshop unless you stood on the window sill and looked through the pine trees to where the hill broke and fell deep down. I used to go there sometimes to pick wild daisies, or to sit on the bare stone ledge of the hilltop. At the bottom among the broken rocks were some rusty machines. That's where my father lay, Uncle Yiftach said, that's where he lay at the bottom of the quarry. On winter nights you could hear the quarry quite clearly. Last winter I couldn't fall asleep because of the voices.

The hill across the quarry is bare, but from the road to the edge of the pit wild flowers grow. I often brought them to Uncle Yiftach and he put them in a jug near the horses, as if they could smell. When the horses were finished, I was the first to ride them. They didn't run far, they really didn't run at all—but if you closed your eyes you could race, you could gallop at breakneck speed to many places, some far from Palestine.

It took Yiftach a long time to finish them; sometimes he worked weeks on just one. Every horse was a different breed.

Since last winter he has finished many new horses, and I have ridden them too, but it is not the same any more. Nothing is the same any more. Elisheva hasn't gone out all year, even though her hair has all grown back. And the British colonel who was in charge of our district no longer shows up. I don't think he ever will again. Hardly anyone does, except once in a while to order a horse from Yiftach.

Last winter a patrol of the British Parachute Division, which came from Cyprus, smashed ten of his horses. It was the second day of the curfew. The soldiers searched the whole place—the cupboards, the beds, everywhere. Elisheva got mad and raised hell, but they wouldn't listen to her. When they were through in the house they went into the workshop, banging their rifle butts on the floor, on the ceiling, everywhere. The sawdust flew, making me sneeze. One of the paratroopers was drunk.

I stood next to Yiftach in the sawdust. I could see the pines through the window. Yiftach held me close while the drunken paratrooper smashed the horses and the others pointed their rifles at us. The drunken paratrooper hit Yiftach and broke his teeth. Yiftach took out a handkerchief and spit a broken tooth into it. The soldiers didn't find anything. When they left, parts of broken horses lay all over the floor. As Yiftach rinsed his mouth out under the tap, I said: "Did he think there was something hidden inside them?"

"No." Yiftach was wiping his face with a towel. "He knew there wasn't."

"I don't think they recognized Elisheva," I said.

"They didn't. They're new here."

Yiftach looked down at the mess on the floor. It was hard to believe these bits and pieces used to be horses. He went over to the corner, lifted up a big block of wood and carried it to the workbench. The wood was rough and knotted, but inside another horse was waiting.

I went out. The soldiers had left by now. Armored British army cars were rumbling up and down the road. I watched them pass by. Then I crossed the road and went to the stone ledge. I sat and looked into the pit. Another group of soldiers went by and I watched them, thinking of the places they'd had to pass before coming here to our small town which—besides thornfields, orange groves, a deserted quarry and a few terrorists who occasionally killed a few English soldiers—had nothing. Then I saw the Colonel's car turn the corner and stop at the gate. I waited a minute, then went back.

The Corporal pinched my cheek and called out: "Hullo, Bobby!" I went into the shop. The Colonel, puffing a pipe, and the Sergeant were looking at the mess. Yiftach was working on the block of wood with his heavy pencil. The Colonel spoke to him, but he didn't turn around. The Colonel looked at the back of Yiftach's neck. Then, taking the pipe from his mouth, he went out, the Sergeant following him. I saw him go up the steps. Elisheva was already waiting at the top. They went inside and the door closed. Now I could see only the two soldiers, the Corporal at the gate and the Sergeant at the foot of the stairs.

"He hasn't been here for a while," I said.

Yiftach turned to me. I knew he didn't want me to look.

"Nadav," and when he opened his mouth I could see the gap left by the broken tooth, "come here." He was standing by the bench. "What are we going to make, Nadav?" His voice was soft, almost a whisper. "We're going to make a new horse, both of us, you and me. Let's see, let's see now. It's not going to be easy," he said. "Not easy at all. He's stubborn, this new fellow, doesn't want to come out. But we'll get him out all right, Nadav, he won't even notice, eh, Nadav?" He winked at me, took his bow saw and tightened the blade. "What's his mane going to look like, Nadav?"

"Tangled."

"Righto, and thick and waving in the wind. And his head?"

"Long."

"And his legs? What will his legs be like, Nadav?"

"Thin."

"Thin, fine and fast as hell. And laugh he will too, won't he? Sure. Oh boy, this one over here is going to be the finest of them all."

He leaned over the block of wood, pulled the carpenter's pencil from his ear and began drawing new lines. I tiptoed on the sawdust to the door. I knew the Sergeant wouldn't let me get by, so I went around by the pines behind the workshop. I went past the big fig tree and the old shed to the terrace at the back. There were an old jerrican, a big jar of black olives, two broken chairs and flowerpots with some dried-up cactus on the terrace. I climbed through without knocking over anything and got into the kitchen.

Elisheva's cat stretched out its neck at me, its whiskers quivering. Yiftach's horses always laughed when they saw me, but never Elisheva's cat. As I came up to her she arched her back and stood there, refusing to budge. I pushed her with my foot: "Bug off." But she only arched her back higher and let out a screech and soon Elisheva came running, in her green silk bathrobe. Elisheva spit her cigarette into the sink and stood there, hands on hips.

"Oh, it's you. Can I help you? Looking for something?"

"Dill pickles."

She just looked at me, and then the Colonel came in too, without his jacket or cap. He smiled and said something I couldn't understand very well, because he spoke English and I didn't understand much English.

"Come on," said Elisheva, picking up the cat. "The Colonel is asking you to join the party."

They took me to the table and the Colonel sat me on his lap, poured out a glass and handed it to me.

I looked at Elisheva.

"The Colonel wants you to drink with him," she said. "Take a sip."

I did.

The drink was bitter. The Colonel smelled of beer and tobacco. His moustache was streaked with silver; two of his teeth were gold. He took out a photograph of a woman and two boys from his wallet and held it up in front of my face.

"His wife and children," said Elisheva. "You see, they're your age."

"Ask him their names," I said.

"John and Pat," said Elisheva, without asking.

"And his wife's name?"

"That's none of your business."

"Where are they?"

"Far away," said Elisheva. "London."

"Yes, London," said the Colonel, twirling his moustache.

"What do they do there?"

"Nothing," said Elisheva. "They just live there."

The Colonel poured another drink. We raised our glasses and clinked them together.

"He's asking if you like John and Pat," said Elisheva.

"They're far away," I said.

I could hear the beer gurgling in his throat as he gulped it down. I raised my own glass to my lips.

"All right, Nadav," said Elisheva. "That will do for today. Another drink and you'll be under the table."

As I got off the Colonel's lap, he gave me his hand. I shook it and said thank you in my best English. Elisheva laughed and said something to him, and the Colonel laughed too. So I said goodbye and took off.

"Wait," said Elisheva.

I stopped.

"Come here, Nadav."

The Colonel took some coins from his pocket and held them out to me. I could see the King looking at me from each of them. I took the coins, put them in my pocket, went out and shut the door behind me.

When she came into my room I was on my bed reading *Pinocchio*. She sat down by my side, the cat in her arms.

"You've been a bad boy, Nadav! That's what you've been." I kept on reading. She said, "There's a curfew and you go out! The British could shoot you down like a mad dog. Don't you know they could? You've been to the quarry again?" I rested the book on my chest. "Why did you go there? I don't want you to go there anymore, you hear?"

"They smashed all the horses," I said.

"Yiftach will make new ones."

"Ten horses," I said. "Ten horse that took Yiftach all summer to make."

"I called the Colonel, didn't I?"

"He came too late."

"He couldn't come earlier."

"He came when they were gone. And they broke a tooth of Yiftach's."

"The Colonel offered to pay for the damage, didn't he? Yiftach shouldn't have snubbed him. King George isn't hard up!"

I picked up my book. She kept on looking at me. When she left I got up and slipped out through the window. He was planing; when I touched his arm he stopped and turned to me.

"Yiftach, why is it no one can show me a photo of my father?"

Yiftach looked at me and then put his fingers in the plane to clear out the shavings.

"Because he didn't leave any photos. That's why."

"Didn't he ever have his picture taken?"

"He did. But he didn't leave any."

Yiftach blew on the plane and I could smell the curly shavings as they fell on the floor. He passed his hand along the blade and sucked his lips.

"Do you think Elisheva burned the photos?"

"I never saw her burn any."

He turned again to the block of wood, and as he planed, legs apart and body moving backward and forward, the sawdust made his blue overalls nearly white.

"What was he like? Did he love her? And did she love him?"

Yiftach let go of the plane and looked at the sweat on the back of his hand.

"My, my. You really are a nosey chap," he said. "Trouble is today is Monday and Monday's a bad day for nosey chaps." He took out a packet of cigarettes. "Let's take the air, eh? Let's go out and have a look at the anemones."

So we went out and sat down by the pines. Yiftach smoked and we looked at the anemones in the field and at the anemones growing into the road. After a while Yiftach put out his cigarette and wiped his hands on his trousers and said:

"Well, that's the way it is."

So we got up and went back into the workshop. I sat on the workbench watching the horse becoming a horse. Then it grew dark outside, and Elisheva called me for supper. After supper the Colonel's car came again, without the Colonel but with the Sergeant. The Sergeant waited on the sofa, playing with the cat, while Elisheva was in her room changing. Yiftach sat in the armchair and gave me a reading lesson. He said it was high time I could read the words, not just the pictures. But I couldn't put my mind to it because of the Sergeant, who kept tickling the cat.

"Why has he come to get her?" I said. "She always goes by herself."

"Because of the curfew," said Yiftach. "They won't let her through."

Elisheva came down, dressed and made up. The Sergeant stood up.

"Mind you don't go to bed late," she said. "I've put out your pajamas. Have some milk if you're thirsty. Not water, you hear? Good night now."

"Good night," I said.

The cat followed them to the door. I stood on tiptoe at the window with my nose pressed against the cold glass. As they walked toward the gate I saw the stars shining in the sky above the pine trees.

"How long will the curfew last?" I said to the windowpane.

"Ask the British High Commissioner, not me," said Yiftach.

"Did they catch many terrorists, do you think?"

"We'll hear on the radio tomorrow."

I watched them get into the car.

"She's a good dancer," I said. "She told me the Colonel loved to dance with her. He gave me money."

"When?" asked Yiftach.

"This morning."

"You shouldn't have taken it."

"Why?"

"You mustn't take money from strangers."

"The Colonel is strangers?"

"Yes, Nadav. He is."

"Then why does Elisheva let him kiss her?"

The car turned the corner and I couldn't see it anymore. I removed my nose from the window pane. Yiftach didn't answer.

"I think I'd better get back to my room," I said.

Yiftach placed his hand on my head and held me close for a while. Then I went to my room, undressed and put on my pajamas. From the window I could see the moon. I could hear the cars cruising up and down the wet road for a long time, then everything was silent. No donkey brayed, no geese cackled, not a dog barked. But in the silence I could hear the quarry and I couldn't fall asleep. I lay wide awake and the quarry wouldn't stop and on and on I heard the quarry, on and on.

In the morning I had a splitting headache. I got up and went into the kitchen. Elisheva was having coffee at the table. Her hair was not brushed; the cat on her lap. I splashed water on my face and sank into my chair. She cut me a slice of bread and gave me a dish of sour cream.

"What was the party like?" I said.

"All right, I guess" she said. "You've got rings around your eyes. Went to bed late?"

I shook my head.

"Then why these rings?"

"Don't know."

"Can't you give me a straight answer?"

"Elisheva," I said, "do you love the Colonel?"

"Beg your pardon?"

"You heard me."

She stared at me. Suddenly her lips tightened and stretched.

"Do you have a temperature?" She placed her hand on my forehead.

I drew back. "Don't."

"Nadav," she said after a pause, "if you finish your cream you'll be as wise as King Solomon and you'll know all the answers and won't have to ask any questions."

"You haven't answered my question."

"Holy Moses!"

She swept out of the room with the cat.

I pushed the dish away and went out to the workshop. A man I didn't know was talking to Yiftach's back. As I walked in the stranger stopped talking and looked at me. The horse was still in the wood, but when I ran my fingers over it I could feel it moving inside.

"That her son?" the stranger asked. He was fat and wore glasses. His big brown beret was pulled down on his forehead, almost over his glasses.

"Hullo," I said, "Cheerio and scram."

"Don't speak English!" said the stranger. "You're Hebrew and your language is Hebrew!"

"Who are you?" I said.

"Nice kid," the stranger said and he tried to pinch my cheek. "But don't you speak English, sonny! English is the language of the enemy."

I turned to Yiftach. "I don't think I know him Yiftach."

"We haven't had an opportunity of meeting," the stranger said.

"What's he want?" I said.

The stranger put his hand on my shoulder.

"Why don't you go and play outside, sonny," he said. "The curfew's over and it's nice outside."

"Just for a few minutes," said Yiftach, looking at me.

The hammock was slung between two pines, but I didn't get into it. I stood by the horseshoes that Yiftach and I had nailed to the trees in summer, for luck.

"Listen, Yiftach," the stranger was saying, "let's not beat about the bush. You know I've come only because you're her brother."

"I'm her brother, all right," I heard Yiftach saying. "A fat lot of good that is."

"Look here, we sent her two letters. We kept warning her we

wouldn't stand by any longer."

I didn't hear Yiftach but I heard the stranger going on:

"The poor kid is a half-orphan already. Why make him a full one? Or does she want to do to him what she did to his father?"

"You talk nonsense," Yiftach said. "She didn't do it to him."

"Sure," the stranger said. "Everybody knows that, but do you want to know what everybody thinks? A man doesn't make a hobby of jumping from great heights into quarries. Somebody has to push him."

"Mister," Yiftach said, and I never heard him speak in such a voice before, "I'm rather busy at the moment!"

There was silence, then I heard the stranger:

"Very well. I've done all I could. All right. But there's one thing I can promise you. Next time there won't be another letter!"

My head was bursting. Thousands of hammers were hammering away inside it. I ran to the quarry and sat on the stone and looked into the pit. I saw the anemones, all around, near and far, a warm red carpet that rustled in the breeze, a forest of soft anemones. From the quarry the voices rose. And in the quarry the old machines stod rusting. The quarry was a deep, deep hole; on its far side were the white rocks of the hill, the hill that had suddenly broken in two and fallen down, into the hole. Only half was left and it was bare: nothing grew on it. And from the hole and from underneath the hole the voices rose.

I lay down on the ground. The soil was wet from the rain and the puddles were filled with silky anemones. I lay on the anemones near the quarry and the sky hung low above me.

It was noon when I went back. The cat was in my chair. As I walked toward it, the cat jumped down and arched against the legs of the chair.

"Wait a minute, Nadav," Elisheva said. I kept looking down at the cat. "Your pants are covered with mud. You've been to the quarry again?" I sat down. "Perhaps we ought to start chaining you to the house like a dog." I looked for the bread. "Haven't I told you a million times not to go there?" I started munching my slice of bread. "All right, go on, don't speak to me. Fine manners you've picked up from that quiet uncle of yours."

"Elisheva," I said. "Are you going to the dance tonight too?"

She gave me a look.

"Yes or no?"

"No."

"Why not?"

"Because there isn't a dance every night."

"Elisheva," I said, "don't see him anymore."

"Him?"

"The Colonel."

"Why?"

I began to gulp my soup. I said nothing.

"All right," she said. "I've heard your reasons. They're not convincing."

"They are."

"They're not."

"They are!"

"They're not!" she said. *"They're not convincing!"* I looked away. *"Absolutely not convincing!"* I kept on gulping. "I thought you were friends. He treats you to beer and gives you money. I thought you were friends."

"We're not."

"So I was wrong." Suddenly she began to laugh. "Look at you," she laughed. "I've given birth to a little terrorist! Perhaps you'll start sending me threatening letters too? I suppose I'm lucky you can't write yet." She pushed aside her plate and got up. "For your information, little terrorist, I'm going to see him soon. I've got a date with him. He will be waiting for me in the Officers' Club. Why not? He's lonely. He can't have his tea without me." She turned, "Come along," she said to the cat. "Let's get dressed."

I finished my soup and took my empty plate and Elisheva's half empty one and put them in the sink. Then I went out to the yard and got into my hammock in the blazing afternoon sun. Elisheva came out wearing her new dress and her jewelry and her white handbag. She didn't speak to me. I didn't speak to her.

I went to my room to read *Pinocchio*. Then I went into the living room where Yiftach was sitting in the armchair reading the evening paper to find out who'd been arrested in the curfew. I went to the window and stood on tiptoe and looked outside. Evening covered the fig tree; the birds had stopped chirping. I could hear the rustling of Yiftach's newspaper as he dropped it on the floor.

"Nadav." But I didn't turn around. "The new horse was waiting for you. He kept on saying: 'Where is Nadav?'"

"He did not," I said.

"You can ask him."

"He said nothing! He can't! He can't speak!"

Yiftach got up and came over to me. I felt his fingers on my shoulder.

"Nadav," he said in his cotton-wool voice. "What's the matter?"

"Nothing." I shook my shoulder. "Nothing, and leave me alone."

He remained standing by me, but his fingers left me. It was just then, when I heard him go back to his armchair, that suddenly I felt the tears well up, and I wasn't even aware how my head all of a sudden found itself on Yiftach's lap.

"She killed him, she killed Father!" I sobbed. "Why did you let her do it, why?"

Yiftach remained silent, my tears splashing on his hand. At last he said:

"The fat man's only a fat man who doesn't always know what he's talking about."

"Then who killed him?"

"No one. The quarry."

His fingers patted my hair. For a long time he sat in silence and I was silent too, and I could feel evening growing tired and making way for night. I looked up.

"Why don't you speak to each other?"

"Nadav," Yiftach said, "when God made people he didn't force them always to talk to each other."

I looked outside. It was pitch dark. She was still not home.

"The Colonel speaks English," I said. "The fat man said English is the language of the enemy."

"The Colonel's an Englishman. Englishmen speak English."

"I saw his children. In the photo. They're the same age as me."

My feet touched the cat's fur. "What do you want? I said. "Elisheva's not here."

"Give her some cheese. She's hungry."

I went to the kitchen, the cat following me, mewing. I took cheese out of the icebox and threw her a few slices. She fell on them and gobbled them up right away. Then she looked back at me and started mewing again.

"Don't be a pig," I said.

I heard the car driving up by the gate, and it didn't sound like the Colonel's car. I ran across the living room to the front window. It was a small truck covered with a tarpaulin. A man jumped from the driver's cabin and let down the tailboard. The tarpaulin was whipped off. Another man jumped out after him. They pulled down something large from the truck and dumped it on the pavement. It was difficult at first to see what it was. The men jumped back into the cabin and the truck drove off. The thing lay still on the pavement, and suddenly I knew. I knew and I screamed:

"YIFTACH! YIF-TACH!" I screamed with all my might: "YIF-TACH! YIF-TACH! Come quick!" Yiftach came running. "She's dead!" I screamed. "They've killed her! They've killed her!"

"Stay here. Don't budge," Yiftach said.

But I couldn't, I just couldn't. I ran after him, the cat after me. Elisheva was crouching, huddled by the gate in the mud, her eyes closed. Her new dress was torn; she held her hands to her head. Her head! It was white; there was no hair on her head. I didn't recognize the head and I didn't recognize Elisheva.

Yiftach bent over her. Her eyes were swollen, her face covered with blood and mud. When he touched her, she started and opened her eyes. She smiled; her smile tore her face apart. In the light of the lamp her eyes were two flakes of mud that had hardened in the sun.

"Good God," I heard him whispering. "What have they done to you?"

Elisheva nodded her shaven head:

"A little beauty treatment," she whispered through her cracked lips.

"Can you get up?"

"What for?"

I could barely hear her, she was speaking so close to the ground. I don't think she saw me. Yiftach made a cradle of his hands beneath her.

"I'm all right here," she said. "Leave me alone here."

"It's all right," said Yiftach. "It's all right."

"Where is the child? Don't let him see me."

"All right."

"Roll me to the quarry, will you? The quarry is deep. Nobody will see, nobody will know. Roll me to the quarry."

He lifted her up and carried her through the gate into the yard. The cat followed them. I saw the light go on in Elisheva's room. I bent down and picked up Elisheva's white bag from the mud. The light from the window lit up the fig tree. I stood for a while and looked up at the window. Then I felt my knees trembling.

Gideon Telpaz was introduced in SSI No. 15 with "My Shadow Rests on Another Wall." Born 1936 in Petah-Tikva, he earned his M.A. at Hebrew University. Mr. Telpaz writes short stories, essays, plays, novels and literary criticism. Five volumes of his short stories have been published in Israel; several of his stories have been translated and published abroad. He has been a visiting professor at universities in the USA and England. Among his awards are the Acum Prize, Anna Frank Prize, Valenrod Prize and a prize for the best original play in 1967 given by the Council for the Arts and Culture.

"I don't wish to defend them,
 but if my head was cut off to be sold to tourists
 I'd know whose fault it was."

Unacceptable Mixture

BY LEOPOLDO CHARIARSE

Scathing humor with imaginative ethnology.

DURING the summer of 1947, in one of the rare moments of lucidity permitted me by the routine of lowly bureaucratic employment, I decided to travel through the Amazon forests, to live in nature, among savages, to learn to handle the bow, to eat unknown animals, fruit of incredible shape, the larvae of insects and the roots of trees never seen.

After a brief stay in Yurimaguas where, despite the suffocating heat, I was able to sleep a little, I took my place in the cabin of the hydroplane that had brought me from Masisea and was to take me to my destination, when a traveler occupying the seat to my right—a bald man, with spectacles and something about him of the attorney or the ecclesiastic—asked me:

"Do you know how many planes have come down this year on our route?"

As I had no idea, I declared brutally:

"Ours will make it a half-dozen."

I told him not to worry, that it was a fair figure, in keeping with the air traffic in that part of the world—one to four per week according to the size of the airline and ours being one of the biggest had more accidents.

My reasoning seemed to offend him. He affirmed that he was not afraid, that he did not need to be calmed down with statistics (for I was explaining that according to the normal curve of accident distribution per unit of time, place, etc.) and that anyway, in spite of completely unfavorable probabilities, it was not death he feared, but desecration of his remains, that at the hands of the savages his flesh might be chopped, ground, salted, or submitted to other treatment incompatible with the dignity of his position.

"I, imagine, a representative of judiciary power, a man without vices, without debts!"

I had to assure him that cannibalism was dying out as evangelization made progress and that after all it was more useful to be eaten by other men than devoured by worms, ants, and piranha.

"Don't be too sure," he exclaimed. "You know very well that in this part of the forest, evangelization has made no progress since the Indians were obliged to work on plantations."

I confined myself to a nod, so as to be able to admire in peace the somber greenery of the forest standing out between the blue and grayish mist over the fiery line of the horizon.

I took a room at a little hotel near the river whose waters I could see from my window stretching away out of sight.

It was a quiet inn; scarcely any travelers were in the lounge and on the terrace, and I was already rejoicing at having come at such a favorable season when deafening cries, rising above the sound of the motor of a big bus, made me see my error.

They were getting out in herds, brandishing their movie and snapshot cameras, photographing in all directions, chewing gum, speaking English, nosily opening and closing doors.

They all asked for precise information on the Maracaburus, while the guide discussed the price of rooms with the proprietress.

I knew vaguely that the Indians of that tribe were the mortal enemies of the Carajones, from whom they had learned, however, the art of preparing a large number of magic philters and subtle varieties of curare. Every month, except during the rainy season, they would come down in their canoes, headed for the village markets along the river bank, to sell their well-known salted meats, their medicinal herbs, and also, though secretly, their poisons that earned them the respect of future inconsolable widows in the area.

While I was telling all this, one of the tourists came up and asked me if they sold shrunken heads here and how high the prices could run.

I was going to reply when the hotel owner, who spoke English too, intervened:

"Here, no. You'll find those in Lima, in stores selling antiques and native curios."

The moment I was preparing to contradict him—for a short distance away, according to what I had been told in Yurimaguas, there was an encampment of Jivaros who kept up a constant trade with the whites, to whom they sold shrunken heads, and with the other Indians from whom they obtained freshly severed ones—he took me by the arm and said to me in an undertone, in Spanish:

"Don't tell them anything. Don't you see that with their mania for carrying off heads they are setting off real massacres among the Indians? For fear of reprisals the latter don't dare refuse to sell any and, as they have none in stock, they are compelled to make them."

"Aren't they stimulated, rather, by profit? No merchant is obliged to meet demand completely," I observed.

"You don't know perhaps, but the Indians remember very well what atrocities were committed against them, when they didn't bring in the rate of rubber the English demanded of them. And now when a gang of Americans come insisting upon having the heads of whites, they fall into a panic and go looking for them where they can. They are dubbed savages for having decapitated a few monks and settlers. I don't wish to defend them, but if *my* head was cut off to be sold to tourists I'd know whose fault it was. The Maracaburus, for example, gentle and peaceable by nature, but tributaries of the Jivaros and obliged to supply them with heads, have become cannibals only so as not to let what remains of their prisoners go to waste.

At that moment a lady interrupted the hotel owner's speech to ask if, further into the interior, it would not be possible for her to obtain a pair of very little heads, children's heads for example, to hang in the rear of her car. White children, she was saying, and French if any could be found. She adored little French children ever since seeing and hearing the "little singers of the wooden cross."

The hotel owner raised his eyes to heaven and left me alone with her. She was a rather fat lady, still young and beautiful. When she spoke there was such enthusiasm in her voice that the sincerity of her love for children could not be doubted.

She told me she belonged to various philanthropic organizations, societies for the protection of animals and waifs and that, in her house in Miami, she had a large collection of tropical fish.

I told her not to worry, that in Lima she would get all the child heads she could wish for, at moderate prices and, who knows, perhaps even French children's heads or Canadian ones from one of the planes come down in the jungle.

I went out that very morning to walk along the river bank. On the right, at the end of an embankment lined with trees, there was a little square in the middle of which, towering above the tops of the coconut palms, rose a sort of column slightly curved. It was an immense cylinder of granite that gave the disorienting feeling of an anachronism or of some monstrous mixture.

Why, indeed, is that phallus—which would not have been out of place in the ruins of Delphi or Mycenae—here, lost in this Christian village on the banks of the Amazon? Was it not an obscure mythological allusion linked with the Amazon seen by Orellana?

Stepping back a little to see from a better angle, I noted that this gigantic member was without its testicles, something that could easily be explained by the prudishness of the authorities. Moreover the glans was missing also, or was hardly indicated perhaps because of a praiseworthy effort at stylization by the artist, tending to anticipate the zeal of an always vigilant censorship.

An inscription similar to that which expresses the public's gratitude to citizens who have fallen at the front only increased my confusion.

It was a monument erected in homage to the martyrs sacrificed by the Maracaburus on the field of honor of Christian faith. There followed a long list of reverend fathers and monks of various orders and numerous military men comprising four lieutenants, fourteen noncommissioned officers, and innumerable soldiers and policemen.

While I was reading the columns set out in strict alphabetical order according to rank, there appeared, dressed all in black, a little old woman making her way sadly but with an indescribably graceful carriage. She approached the railing protecting the monument and dropped a few flowers near the plaque, into a sort of metal box put there for that purpose. Seeing her, I thought I could hear a military band in the distance and a feeling of great tenderness would have come over me if, raising my eyes to the sky, I had not seen that inexorable shape defying all pity.

A most passionate interest followed my initial curiosity upon seeing the old woman's hair combed in a manner that brought to mind irresistibly a Greek hairstyle.

I approached her—a bacchante or a weeping figure exiled at the foot of this last vestige of her divinity—and, to say something, asked her—this is explained by my complete confusion—what day it was and the name of that place.

"Martyrs' Square," she said smiling and she added, "Every time I come back here, it seems I am going mad. I couldn't tell you what day it is, Sir. Excuse me."

Back at the hotel I demanded that the proprietress tell me for what reason, in Martyrs' Square, a pagan sign commemorated the death of these holy men.

She explained that this monument did not represent a male member at all but a sausage.

Faced with my amazement, the good woman confirmed:

"It's because of the victims transformed into sausages by the Maracaburus.

"The best pork-butchers in the area," added the proprietress' husband who was reading a newspaper, his elbows on the counter.

"Did that event take place a long time ago?" I asked with a certain uneasiness, irritated by the hotel owner's remark.

"Exactly three years," he replied, giving up reading. "Since then the hamlet of Maracaburu, a couple of miles from here, is one of the most prosperous places of pilgrimage in the whole country. During the busy season, we don't have enough room to put up all the pilgrims."

"In spite of the new hotel that's been built," added the hotel owner's wife bitterly. "Just imagine, we have to put mats and hammocks out, even in the dining room!"

At lunch, I was introduced to Father Saravia. The hotel proprietor told him I had arrived from Lima and did not know the story of the miracle that the martyrs' remains had occasioned.

"Don Pedro Irribáuregui—a relative of mine—had just been appointed bishop of the region," said the father, "when he summoned me to come immediately so that he could ask me to inquire into an event of which the theological and practical implications presented the most unreal and grotesque appearance.

"It had been discovered that a group of Maracaburu Indians had cut up and mixed the flesh of numerous priests, soldiers, and policemen with that of pigs and dogs stolen from the farms in neighboring villages. I had to find out how it was possible to grant those remains Christian burial and, first of all, establish if such a thing had been possible."

A captain traveling in the direction of the frontier sat down at our table. Of indeterminate age, but fitting his uniform perfectly, he greeted us in friendly fashion, declared that his name was Mirasoles and that he was a member of a commission charged with determining where the frontier ran, through zones about which the treaties in force left some doubt. It was certainly not the least curious aspect of the question to see the two countries in dispute over regions inhabited by cannibal tribes, each claiming the land but affirming that the cannibals were natives of the neighboring country. This contradiction and others I could not grasp very well made the captain's work extremely tiring and complicated.

When the captain learned from the hotel owner's wife, who had come up to wait on us, that Father Saravia had begun to tell me a story, he asked to be excused for interrupting us and wanted to move to another table, but we invited him to stay, telling him there was nothing secret about this story and that he could, in fact, be useful to us in clarifying certain details.

He accepted gratefully and we prepared to listen to the rest of the tale.

"As I was saying," the priest went on, "the problem was agonizing. Could Christian burial be given remains in which it was impossible to distinquish the human from the animal, not to mention other ingredients it would be too painful to speak of."

"That's the easiest thing in the world," declared the soldier to whom every problem seemed simple. "All they had to do was determine the exact amount of each part of the mixture and divide each sausage accordingly, symbolically bringing together the parts corresponding to the clergy, the army, and the animal kingdom, and bury them separately, even though in reality the mixture was inextricable. It was all a matter of establishing the proportions exactly."

"You've said it: that was the whole problem. But the Maracaburus, jealous of their manufacturing secrets and fearing that other tribes might appropriate these and cut them out of the market, would rather let themselves be killed than reveal them."

"But how was it known that the Maracaburus' sausages were made of human flesh?"

"A few missionaries having disappeared, someone remembered that a comparable event had taken place about fifty years before, when the Dominicans found themselves obliged to change the route they used to take to reach their missions in Brazil. There resulted such a famine among the Indians, for whom they were the staple diet, that very few survived."

"I know," interjected the captain. "Driven by hunger, they crossed the frontier and began attacking villages and plantations. They'd have got as far as Iquitos if they'd not been stopped by the heroic resistance of our troops who, aided by the settlers, in the end exterminated them."

"To get back to my story, when the disappearances reached alarming proportions, the police scoured the whole region in question but with no other result than the disappearance of numerous policemen."

"That's when the army stepped in," exulted Mirasoles, filling out his uniform once again so that it seemed to have more buttons than ever.

"The result was the disappearance of almost a whole regiment," the priest continued imperturbably.

I thought of that little old woman's flowers and those four lieutenants, fourteen noncommissioned officers, and I don't know how many soldiers mentioned on the plaque that seemed to me terribly human, almost familiar.

But the captain replied:

"All the same, it was thanks to us that the Indians confessed to having killed the missionaries."

"Finally the dreadful version of the facts had to be admitted and some Indians confessed, spontaneously or out of fear of being interrogated, that they had taken part in the massacre."

"Immediate seizure of the meat brought in by the savages was then decreed," thundered Mirasoles again, taking the opportunity to explain his role in detail. "At that time I was just a lieutenant," he said modestly.

With dinner behind us, we went to sip coffee on the terrace. The man in spectacles, who knew Mirasoles and Saravia, came up to our table and joined in the conversation. We felt he was very agitated. He told us he had received several threatening letters over a case involving tradespeople, in which he was to act as mediator.

Father Saravia went on:

"As soon as confiscation had been completed in fairs and markets, interment of the remains was carried out, with no distinction, in a common grave, and the names of the victims were inscribed on a plaque. Mgr. Irribáuregui, who presided over the ceremony, pronounced a moving eulogy. He deplored the absence of the heads and regretted there was no hope of retrieving them, for the Jivaros were uncompromising and it would have been necessary to buy a large quantity from them to separate the heads of civilized people and identify them. This obviously called for special government funds and the cooperation of all the faithful in the province. He would take this matter up: he was counting on the understanding of the government and the generosity of all."

On the morning of the third day the grave was found to be open and there was complete consternation when it was known that the remains had disappeared. A mixture of terror and indignation ran through clergy and settlers. The military and the police were placed on alert. A curfew was imposed and several Indians shot down in the vicinity.

"The massacre threatened to imperil the whole district's economy if the native population, which does the heavy work and constitutes the main tourist attraction, was decimated," Mirasoles observed pertinently.

"Divine mercy," Saravia continued, "permitted a group of Indians to manage to get to the bishop and relate the event they had all witnessed. Returning to their huts, a little after midnight, they said, a blinding light took them by surprise and while the night was rent by lightning and trumpet music, they had seen the tomb open and the sausages rise up to heaven."

Mgr. Irribáuregui gave up his return flight to Iquitos that day, and, calling together clergy and people of standing, solemnly announced the miracle.

Great festivities were organized and, to everyone's joy, the Indians who were to be executed for having participated in the massacres and in salting the meat were allowed to escape. The erection of a monument was decided upon immediately and Mgr. Irribáuregui insisted upon its being given the shape of a sausage.

"Out of respect for his dignity as a prelate and his venerable age we accepted this idea that seemed to us absurd and terribly ridiculous. To our timid objections he replied that it would be a lesson in modesty to the flesh and an example of what man is capable of who has entered the bosom of Christianity."

Time has borne out what the bishop said, for the number of

pilgrims has not stopped rising from year to year and there is already talk of building a basilica.

His story over, Father Saravia consulted his watch, declared he had to go to work, and left.

Scarcely had he gone when the man with spectacles turned to me and, with a sinister air, said:

"What the good priest doesn't know is that the next day, in all the markets and shops selling food, the famous sausages appeared once again. Housewives were buying them, we were eating them, and no one thought that those who claimed to have witnessed a miracle were the same ones who had sold them. Serious rivalry between tradespeople allowed me to learn the truth. In my capacity as magistrate I did all I could to conceal it, so as to avoid a scandal, but the explosion is inevitable."

Born 1928 in northern Peru, Leopoldo Chariarse studied ethnology, then philology in Barcelona, then musicology in Paris. His imagination and powerful black humor are saluted especially by surrealists. J.H. Matthews, translator of "Unacceptable Mixture," is an editor, professor of French and a perceptive historian and critic of surrealism.

"We've got a volcano underneath us
and the British Government on top."

Stresspoint

BY COLIN BEADON

Drama and decisions at a drilling site.

IT was the middle of August. There was no afternoon wind along the tops of the mountains and no clouds in the sky. The sun hung like an angry blow-torch above the valley where the rig stood and the usually dark green richness of the bush had turned to the brown and the dead and the dusty, and the black where fire had been.

The drilling contractor worked in the trailer "Doghouse." He had stripped to his waist and was sweating heavily in the Caribbean pre-rain heat, writing a report on a driller he had had to fire for coming to work drunk on two occasions. As sweat dripped from his face he blotted it away with a Kleenex to keep the report as neat as possible.

There was a knock on the door. He turned from the desk and looked up at the rig through the open windows. They were down two thousand feet and drilling. The satisfying pulsing "thud" of the big downhole pumps came up through the doghouse flooring.

"Come on in."

A black man stepped on the rung of the ladder and blotted the light from the doorway.

"Yes?"

"I'm Baily," the man said in a rusty voice. He was an elderly man with a deeply lined face, a gray stubble of beard and a battered steel helmet. "They sent me up to replace Drayton." He slid a company envelope to the table with great calloused lightly trembling hands.

The drilling contractor removed his sunshades. There were white circles around his eyes where the shades kept the sun from his face. There was the drawn and haggard look from too much loss of sleep. He looked puzzled.

"They sent you up? I don't get it. I told them I didn't need anybody."

"They told me get to St. Lucia," the man called Baily said. "They gave me a ticket and a tax clearance." He was standing awkwardly, his huge hands on the back of the seat across from the drilling contractor's desk.

"You'll have to go on back. I'm not going to make promotions over the men I got here. They've been with me a year. They know the set-up. I told Trinidad I didn't need anybody."

The drilling contractor went back to his report. Baily stood silently in the Doghouse. Three minutes went by.

"I need the work," he said sullenly.

The drilling contractor looked up with his tired green-slate eyes with crow's feet deepening the corners. He seemed to suddenly recognize this man for the first time.

"I don't need anybody and that's final." He went on with his report.

"A chance Mr. Bronson."

The drilling contractor kept on writing.

"Tell me," he said, still writing, "did Timothy get out of hospital?"

"No," said Baily.

"Did he lose the arm?"

"Yes," said Baily. "It wasn't my fault. It was bad luck."

"I don't need that around," said the drilling contractor. "There's a flight in the morning."

"It wasn't my fault." Baily lit a cigarette. His hands trembled badly now.

"It's never anybody's fault. That's all you ever hear. I've got green St. Lucian floorhands. I can't take a chance."

"You can't take a chance on forty years oilfield experience?"

"This isn't the oilfields. This is steam. You've got to learn some of it over again."

"I won't have a job if I go back," said Baily. "Ive got eleven children. Nine in school."

"I suppose that wasn't your fault either," said the drilling contractor. He looked out the window up on the rig floor. The crew were making a connection (joining a new joint of drillpipe to what was in the hole).

Baily turned away and stood in the doorway looking up at the rig. He looked at it like a man looks at something he has known and loved for the whole of his life. The drilling contractor caught that gaze like a man catches the look in the eyes of a woman who has fallen in love with him.

"Jesus Christ. All right. All right," he broke. "I'll try you. Get some rest and come out daylight tomorrow. This is a day-rate contract. Not footage. Take your time and for shit sake don't foul up. That's all I ask. We've got a perfect safety record and we've got mostly green hands. We've got a volcano underneath us and the British Government on top. One fuckup is all we need."

"As long as I get a good derrickman," Baily said.

"You're asking a lot. You're lucky. You'll get Simms. He's the best there is."

"That's all I need," said Baily.

"That's not all you need. You need to keep the hole full at all times, and if you are losing fluid, never stop pumping. If you stop pumping, shut the rams. The well will give you three minutes without pumping and she'll be around your neck. Don't ever forget it. Because it will be the last thing you'll ever have to forget."

119

Baily grinned, stooped under the Doghouse doorway and went out into the bright sun. He stood looking up at the rig. He had status now. He got into the taxi that had brought him from the airport and went back down the slope from the location past the volcano and on down along the mango tree lined road that wound through the mountains and dropped into the town that lay in the bay of Soufriere.

George Spencer came sweat-dripping into the Doghouse. His shirt was stained with it and his pants where his belt should have been and stained around his crotch. His black face shone with sweat.

"Where did they get him?" he asked.

"Unloading him I guess," said the drilling contractor. "He's too old. Watch him."

"Just what we need," said George Spencer, going to the fridge. "He should have been out of it five years ago."

"They'll be saying that of us one day," said the drilling contractor, running his hand through his receding graying hair. "We'll try him. Warn Blade when he comes in the morning."

"He's too old Mr. Bronson. You've worked too hard putting this contract together, building the rig, floating her from Trinidad, humping her up the mountains."

"I wouldn't have done it without help," said the drilling contractor twisting the wedding band on his finger.

"True. But you. You've sunk everything into it. It's a wildcat contract and you've taken the chance of life time and the gamble of the century and probably every cent you ever worked for. You going to chance it on a bad card now? You've got the people of this island to think of too. They need that power source. A megawatt and a half will save them two million a year in fuel, and that's only today's price. How will they buy diesel tomorrow?"

"You don't know the whole story," said the drilling contractor. He was twisting the wedding band on his finger.

"It would have to be a good one," said George Spencer.

"How about I owe him my life?"

"I see," said George Spencer slowly. He sat down.

"It was a blow-out one night in Grande Ravine. I got gassed and went out. I'd only been on a rig a couple of weeks. When everyone got clear of the well and found me missing, he came back in, found me somehow and carried me out. She ignited a few moments after he got me clear. It was a bad one."

"OK, so he's your hero. He, he's an old man now. You haven't been hearing about him recently."

"I've heard."

"If you've heard, you're mad."

"Who isn't in the drilling industry?"

"Two men got killed with him last year," George Spencer insisted.

"That wasn't his fault."

"It's always your fault. What about Timothy last month in Trinidad?"

"I know. I know."

"As long as you know. How we going to keep him awake on the night shift?"

"Some old men don't sleep."

"Only the bad."

"You won't sleep when you're his age," said the drilling contractor laughing.

"Not if I have a young woman," said George Spencer taking a long gulp of cold water and wiping his mouth on his shirt tail. "A make or break like this and you're going to throw bad dice. As if we didn't have enough catchass already. When did you last sleep a full night?"

"My wife hasn't arrived," said the drilling contractor twisting his wedding band again. George Spencer looked at him closely.

"Anyhow the British are pleased enough. They say it's the best project of its kind they've done in years."

"That's just what I mean," said George Spencer. He took another gulp of ice water.

"We'll keep an eye on him."

"We have enough to keep our eyes on. Three close calls so far. I.G.S. don't know what we're liable to meet and when you see a geologist sweating, Hombre, watch out."

"Did you hear the news today? The volcano in Guadeloupe is

erupting. The St. Lucians are saying it's because we're drilling
here. They're worried.''

"Well you know that's bull," said the drilling contractor.

It was seven in the morning and the clouds stood dark and
massing like a great army above the line of the mountains. It was
still and oppressive and from far out to sea came the first rumble of
thunder in the eye of the storm.

There were women, heads heaped with produce, coming down
the mountains to the rig location that met the road which led to the
town. An old man goaded a fat pig. A fresh young girl milked a
bleating goat to one side of the location upon which the rig sat. In
the little wooden shacks women and children shook the cock-
roaches from pans and drums in readiness for the rain. A dog
chased a young fighting cock that took to the air and flew over the
drillingpipe racks and high into a breadfruit tree trumpeting in
clarion-like defiance.

The rig crew were making a "trip" to change a dull bit. Drillpipe
stood steaming in the derrick. They had fifteen hundred feet out
now and another seven hundred to pull. Each time the block came
back and they latched the elevator on the next stand, the small rig
dipped lightly with the load as she took the weight.

The fresh tool pusher now on duty stood on the mud tank
walks. He was measuring the drilling fluid being pumped into the
hole as it took the place of the drillpipe being pulled out. They
were on a slight fluid loss to the formation and it was to be expected now as they had just entered the steam zone. The tool pusher
had to be sure that the hole was staying full and that there was no
indication of it trying to start flowing on its own. This was a critical
stage, but this morning he had more concern over a driller.

The tool pusher called Blade jumped from the tank walks when
he saw the drilling contractor's white Dodge nose on to the location. He found the contracor reading the night's report.

"Where did they get the old man?" he asked.

The contractor read on as though he hadn't heard. A pre-rain
breeze came into the Doghouse.

"What's wrong with him?"

"He's giving me horrors," said Blade. " I don't think he can see up the derrick."

"He's been at it so long he doesn't need to see up there. Give him a chance. He'll settle down."

"Six foot down, or he'll put some of the men there. He's giving me cold sweat. Take a look for yourself. I'm going back on the tanks."

The drilling contractor went on with his scrutiny of the report. He placed a red mark against Caustic and Bentonite. He would have to re-order for the following wells. He poured coffee, added milk and sugar. He sipped cautiously and made a face. Standing at the doorway he watched the driller at the draw-works controls. A frown spread over his face. Coffee cup in hand he walked across the location and up the ladder to the floor.

"Mr. Baily. A bit more care if you please."

"I'm not used to a crew like this," Baily said stubbornly.

"That's why I request a little more care."

"Right Boss, right."

The contractor turned on his heels and went back to the Doghouse. He had just entered when there came the sudden clash of gladiator-like steel followed by an unnerving quick-choked shout; and hot coffee went down his shirt unfelt.

Derrickman in a safety harness hanging like a spider on a twelve-foot thread. Driller leaning over the draw-works brake, squinting into the derrick. Three floor crew in an upward facing freeze. Headman shaking his head, a stunned deathlike grin on his face. Derrickman turning slowly, dazed, winded, shocked, help-less, sixty feet above the steel floor, a brown watery stinking fluid running out of his trouser legs, hanging like a slipped climber over the edge of a precipice. Rain coming lightly with the wind, and then harder, and then in a tropical storm.

"Chain her down and don't touch anything," the drilling con-tractor shouted. He was scrambling for the ladder like a fighter pilot goes for his cockpit. Blade was two paces ahead of him. They both climbed with swift accustomed ease and then they were treading carefully out along the rackingboard to stand above the man who hung limply in the rain.

There was little room for one man to stand and take the weight of the man who hung like a spider twelve feet below. The drilling contractor braced himself against the outer rail, set his feet and took hold of the rope. He picked up about two feet when he straightened his back, but before the tool pusher could make the wrap, the wet rope slid back through the hands of the drilling contractor, burning him as it went and whereas he wanted to let it go, he stood and took it as it slid and burnt his hands as it went. When the weight of the man was back on the rail, he let go, looked at his hands quickly and placed them under his wet armpits like a man tries to warm in winter.

"You're stronger than I am," he said to the young black tool pusher called Blade. "See if you can hold him while I take the slack. Wrap that cloth in your pocket around your hands."

"It's full of dieseline and grease," Blade said. "Let me have a go anyhow."

They changed positions. Blade set back and braced himself against the weight of the man who hung below too frightened to move. The racehorse-like chest and arm muscles jumped in the rain as he took the load like a man breaking out a bottom-bound anchor.

Foot by foot they worked that man back to safety. Then they had him up on the rackingboard and then there was the close embrace that men have held each other in through since the dawn of mankind when just after the hand of death has been played and lost. Sims stood with his eyes closed. He trembled uncontrollably standing between the two men who had helped him back. Somehow the rain had stopped and one bright shaft of sunlight split through the clouds and lit them for a moment. And then it was gone.

"You're all right now. Breathe deeply. You're safe now," the drilling contractor said.

The derrickman mumbled something unintelligible. They nursed him step by step to the ground. They shouldered him to the Doghouse and got him on to a bunk. There was blood in his armpits where the safety belt had bit with the jolt. Blade poured water into a glass and had him take some of it.

"Stay with him," said the drilling contractor. He went out the door.

"I'm afraid that's it," said the drilling contractor not unkindly. The old driller straightened up from over the draw-works brake where he had been leaning and waiting. He looked quite lost. Uncertainly he said, "I don't know what happened."

"You mistimed him. Luckily it wasn't too serious."

The old driller had his great hand clamped tight on the draw-works brake as though he knew that once he let go, it would be the last time he would hold a "pigfoot."

"I'm sorry. I can't keep you on," the drilling contractor said. He placed a friendly hand on the hollowing back. The old driller slowly released his grip. And then, he turned away and went down the ladder.

The drilling contractor took over the controls like he had relieved a man who wanted to crap. The headman was up the derrick buckling on the harness.

"You ready Steadman?"

"Go ahead Boss."

They racked back the stand of drillpipe that had knocked the derrickman into space. It started raining again.

The old driller came out of the Doghouse holding his wet work clothes. He still had on his helmet.

"When is the next plane?" he called from the ground behind the contractor.

"You should make the four o'clock. Eastern Airways. Call from the hotel if you want. Time to put away that hat old man. Good luck now."

The old driller went down the location in the torrent, walking aimlessly without turning back.

The drilling contractor called the tool pusher.

"Take them both to town. Get him transport for the airport and take Sims to the Doc."

"I feel bad for him," said Blade.

"Me and my soft heart," muttered the contractor.

"You gave him a chance," said Blade going for his car.

The contractor went on with the work. By the time the tool pusher arrived back, they had the bit on the "bank" and were making up the new one to run in the hole.

"He got away OK?"

"Not yet. I set up transport for midday and checked he had his papers and everything."

"How was he taking it?"

"A bottle of rum."

"Shit! He deserves whisky. The best that money can buy," said the drilling contractor.

"That won't help him tomorrow."

"One day at a time. That's all he's got left."

"And us? How long we got?"

"As long as it takes," said the drilling contractor, twisting the wedding band on his finger.

At fourteen years of age, in 1949, Colin Beadon came to Trinidad where his father was posted as police chief. "School was a dead loss." At seventeen, he went to sea for three years and has since worked in oilfields in Venezuela, St. Lucia and Trinidad. Greatly influenced by his Aunt Cecilie Leslie, an author, Mr. Beadon says: "I'd love to only write, but I know I need the boost and thrash of the external world and all its joy and pain." He proclaims his greatest backstay to be his wife and "two good strong wild sons, and the fact that we all love ocean cruising under sail, fishing and loud music."

"There was stunned silence,
  broken only by the eruption into pious ejaculations
  of the lady who was fingering the rosary."

Eccentric Ferns

BY PETER NAZARETH

A non-conformer in a church-going community.

THE Goans of Apana thought that Horace Fernandes was a strange fellow. It was not that he was unfriendly—on the contrary, he seemed to be at ease with everybody he met. The trouble was that he paid no attention to the rules of society. He did not visit people according to the unwritten schedule, he did not make calls of homage on the Goan elders, that is, the Goans who were high up in the Civil Service.

The worst thing of all was that he was not God-fearing. He did not frequent the Church. On Sundays, it was said, he merely slept at home until very late, although some people claimed that they sometimes saw him sitting at the back of the Church and muttering to himself. In the days when eating meat on Friday was a mortal sin, he ate meat on Friday. When somebody had challenged him about committing a mortal sin by indulging his appetite, he was said to have replied that the ancient Roman Catholic

Church had only made it a sin to eat meat on Fridays because there had been an excess of fish on the Roman market, and this was a way of ensuring that people bought fish! Fernandes was a common name, but this was an uncommon fellow! Everybody said that this one was eccentric, and he acquired the name Eccentric Fernandes, which eventually became Eccentric Ferns.

Lately, he had got worse. Word started going round that he had joined some mysterious religious order. What was to be done?

Some pious old ladies decided to take it upon themselves to try and save him.

The statue of the Blessed Virgin Mary used to be taken from house to house, to the accompaniment of a group of people singing hymns, where it used to have pride of place in the sitting room and where the family of the house was supposed to pray and put money in the box keeping vigil over Our Lady. Eccentric Ferns had always refused to take the statue. The ladies now had a bright idea. They arranged for the statue to go to Ferns's neighbors just before these neighbors and those on the other side of his house were to go away for the weekend. They then approached Ferns and said that his neighbor was going away and, as there was no one else available nearby until the other neighbors returned, could he please take the statue for a day? He said no, he was very sorry, he would not as he did not worship idols. They kept on pleading, for they had faith in Our Lady: once She was in his house, She would save him. Finally, he agreed to help them, but he said that he would have no prayers and no singing of hymns, and he would lock the statue in the storeroom instead of keeping it in the living room. The ladies agreed; Our Lady was beginning to answer their prayers. Unfortunately, he did just what he had said—when he went to collect the statue from his neighbor, he covered it with a cloth, sneaked it into his house, and locked it in the storeroom until it could be taken away.

The ladies did not give up. They decided to go to his house and try to reason with him. Horace Fernandes met them very politely at his door, showed them into the sitting room and offered them some tea. He listened very patiently while they evoked words like Humility before God and Thanking God for the Gifts He had given Mankind. One of the ladies sat silently in the corner, fingering the beads of her rosary. Finally, he said:

"Ladies, thank you for being so concerned about me. I am really touched that you have made such an effort, and I respect your beliefs. Why don't we agree that you believe what you want to believe and I believe what I want to believe?"

"How can that be?" one of the ladies burst out. "There is only one true God!" Then, in an effort to quote the Bible, she made a reference to "those perfidious Jews." Horace Fernandes's patience seemed to have been strained to its utmost.

"Why condemn the Jews?" he said. "Jesus was a Jew, not a Christian. He said that He did not come to cast out the old religion. In any case, like every good Jew, He was circumcised."

There was stunned silence, broken only by the eruption into pious ejaculations of the lady who was fingering the rosary. Finally, one of the bolder ones said: "Well! And that is what comes of an unholy man who is known to consort with loose women! The Pope—"

"I do not necessarily attach value to what a Pope says," said Ferns. "There was a Pope Alexander in the fifteenth century who had illegitimate daughters, and who had relations with one of these daughters." The lady with the rosary stood up. Ferns said that he was surprised that such pious ladies were shocked at what he had said. After all, wasn't there somebody in the Bible who had children by his daughters?

The ladies fled. After that, they stayed away from his house but decided to offer masses for him.

In keeping with the changes taking place in the Church, the parish priest had introduced a scheme of inviting priests from the neighboring parishes to deliver a sermon during Sunday mass. The usual priest would say the mass, and after the gospel, the visitor would come forward and deliver the sermon.

On the Sunday on which the third mass was offered for Eccentric Ferns, the visiting priest did not turn up on time. The people waited impatiently while the priest who was saying the mass fidgeted on his seat, wondering whether he should deliver an impromptu sermon.

Ah, there he was! The visiting priest. He mounted the pulpit.

"My dear brethren," he began, "Do unto others as you would have them do unto you. Words from today's gospel. Have we ever paused to meditate on what these profound words of Christ mean? Now, on this special occasion, fifty days after the Ascension of Christ, let us dedicate ourselves anew to asking ourselves what these words of Christ mean.

"What they mean, my dear brethren, is that we must appreciate most fully this wonderful sacrifice of the mass. Think what a great gift our good Lord has given us! For without the wonderful sacrifice of the mass, how would we feel connected with the Divine Self, with our Creator? How would we find ourselves devoting at least one day of each week to GOD? We, sinners as we are, do not realize the great gifts God has given us."

The people were staring fixedly ahead, thinking their various thoughts. A few were dozing.

"Ah!" said the preacher "Just as I thought. You come to Church every Sunday in your finest clothing and do not pay the slightest attention to what is going on. To you, God is a kind of business partner, who would withdraw his investment if he is not humored at least once a week. Automatic machines, sleepwalkers, that's what you are! For the last few minutes I have been uttering totally disconnected words, and you have not noticed!

"Do you know, friends, most of my fellow-priests have a Do-it-Yourself Sermon Kit. Each kit contains phrases and expressions written out on cards. My colleagues know that you do not pay any attention to what they say, so before each mass, they merely pick out a few cards—and there is a sermon!"

By now, the congregation was wide awake. Even the priest saying the mass looked surprised.

"Let us think for a change," said the preacher, "of what Christ really said. Do unto others as you would have them do unto you—not words from today's gospel, but words that Christ uttered all the same. You will notice that Christ did not say do unto Christians as you would have them do unto you—he said unto others. This means that we should treat all our fellow-humans humanely, even if they do not believe in the Church! For example, instead of putting money into the Church collection plate to build even bigger Churches and Cathedrals, we should give our money to feed the poor. Better still, we should help the poor by working to build them places of shelter, helping them to find employment and to look after themselves. For all people need to have pride and self-respect.

"Why do we need so many Churches and statues? Did Christ spend all his time in Churches and Temples? Did he show any interest in statues such as adorn this Church? Did he set aside fixed days and forms of prayers and condemn those who did not follow the pattern? Does the parable of the Good Samaritan teach us that only Christians are good people? Humbug, HUMBUG, to say that this is what Christ stood for!"

The congregation sat goggle-eyed. At that moment, another priest walked in.

One person could not contain himself but said: "Eccentric Ferns! That's who he is! That man is no priest!"

Yes, it was indeed Horace Fernandes! The priest and the elders of the congregation shot up and closed in on the pulpit. Horace seemed to lose his self-control for the first time.

"Christ, bear witness!" he shouted. "This Church is not yours! In your name the imperialists held an inquisition in Goa and tortured and killed our ancestors. Others fled to other parts of India, where there were truly Christian people, who had never heard of Christianity . . ."

By that time, several people had climbed into the pulpit to eject Eccentric Ferns. The pulpit had been made for the congregation but not for the congregation to be on it: it collapsed. The people all spread out in a heap on the floor. In the confusion, Eccentric Ferns made his escape. Fortunately, the only injuries were to the people's dignities.

How had Eccentric Ferns known that the visiting preacher would have a breakdown on the way and not reach the Church on time? How had he managed to put on a priest's cassock without the sacristan seeing him?

The old ladies stopped offering masses for Eccentric Ferns.

Sometimes the Devil cannot be beaten.

Peter Nazareth was born and raised in Uganda. His parents had emigrated from Goa, a part of India. When Idi Amin came to power, people of Nazareth's background were deprived of their citizenship and forced to leave Uganda. He is presently in the USA teaching East African literature on the college level, and writing. His "main audience is in East Africa and also West Africa." Most of his works are published in East African journals. The Third World Writer, *a book of literary criticism, is his latest publication.*

"As he watched them, Mike wondered
what the future held for them all and what
could be done for Little Banana."

The Future of Little Banana

BY KEVIN COSTELLO

Parents learn the truth about their child.

BIG Mike shifted the baby from one shoulder to the other while
Angie fumbled in her purse for the appointment slip. He looked at
the crowd of children and parents lining the wall and knew there
would be a long wait. Little Mike was restless and Big Mike knew
that as soon as they joined the throng of children along the wall
that one of them would begin to cry and Little Mike would wail in
soul-rending counterpoint.

"Migulito never cries, except when he hears other children
crying. He's a real sympathetic type," Mike would explain often to
anyone who would listen. He was aware as he said it that he
sounded like a typical fatuous father, but he had decided that he
would rather sound like a fatuous father than a phlegmatic grandfather. At 42, he could have been the baby's grandfather, and
Angie, at 36, could have been a grandmother. In Tennessee, or
Bali, or *someplace.*

"Take a seat and your name will be called," said a nurse, whom Mike immediately described to himself as "crisp, starched and efficient," as though one of the editors who had interviewed him were listening to his thoughts. He felt that if this *were* the case, any such editor would be reassured that he was a safe element, unlikely to clutter up his copy with multi-level *esoterica,* upstaging the regular columnists, a docile workhorse with the proper cliché. He did not believe that any of the editors he had seen had even listened to his pitch, and the game of thinking in clichés for their benefit soon lost its amusement value. The feeling of frustration that he had worn like a tight headband since his arrival in San Francisco now engulfed him like a shroud as he carried the wriggling baby to a seat along the wall.

He had known when he left Mexico City that San Francisco was the last city in the world to arrive C.O.D. with a wife and a sickly child, expecting to land a job on a newspaper. One of the wire stories he remembered was the merger of the *News* and *Call-Bulletin,* and a few years later the demise of the new hybrid. At the time of the original merger, he had just moved over to the English desk on *El Universal,* and was feeling pretty secure, but he could sympathize with all the men who were sitting at their desks in San Francisco, looking at one another and wondering who was going to get jettisoned. He knew that a lot of them were thinking, heart-in-throat, of the one cliché they all had used, but had never sent downstairs, the one they might have used, unwittingly in the presence of the very man who was sitting in the front office, his pencil poised over a list of names. This cliché might even now be tipping the scales for some of them, and it goes like this: *"If I'd had any guts (sense, moxie, intelligence) five years ago, I'd have quit this stinking (chicken-shit, lousy, stupid) rag, and gotten myself a real (decent, normal, legitimate) job on a ranch (in a brewery, in a brassiere factory, in a whore-house)."*

When the *News-Call-Bulletin* finally folded, he wondered where the staff wound up, whether they fanned out over the city and became waiters and bartenders, trying to remain in "Everybody's Favorite City," and then, despairing, dispersed throughout the country, or whether there was a Sargasso Sea of newspapermen somewhere. *That's a terrifying idea,* he thought, amused, *imagine all the cast-off dingalings in this racket in the same place!* His amusement was short-lived as Angie said, "Here, let me take him. You're carrying him like a sack of coal." He surrendered the baby without protest, because he *did* feel that he carried it awkwardly, although he loved the feel of the little body in his arms. He made a mental note to ask Angie where the hell *she'd* ever seen anyone carrying a sack of coal. Born in L.A. and raised in Guadalajara, she'd never even seen a *lump* of coal, probably. He watched her maneuver through the crowd and squeeze into a place on one of the benches. He followed her over and stood above her in a tableau reminiscent of subway passengers of his New York youth.

A little girl with a bandaged arm and a tear-stained face became interested in Little Mike, and Mike hoped that whatever the fascination was, it was sufficient to keep her from crying again for a while longer. There were about fifteen children in the corridor, and it seemed mathematically probable that at least *one* of them would be crying at any given moment. Or rather, at least *two* of them, since Little Mike would share the Wailing Wall on cue with both prince and urchin.

Angie busied herself with the baby's snow-suit, opening the hood and peeling it down around him, leaving only his little feet enclosed. She chattered to him incessantly. "See, *Miguelito,* I peel you like a banana. Oh, I love you Little Banana."

As he watched them, Mike wondered what the future held for them all and what could be done for Little Banana. He was premature, and at nine months did not seem to be progressing as quickly as the doctors who attended his delivery at the American Hospital in Mexico had said he would. They did say that he would require a lot of attention and this was the factor that had brought him back to the States with the problem, a variation on the theme of back-to-the-womb or back-to-the-cave.

On the credit side, Angie had fallen in love with San Francisco so it was not as though he had dragged them into some whistle-stop by the scruff of the neck to work out their salvation. Personal preference had not been a factor in his choice of battlegrounds.

His only living relatives were two sisters whom he had urged to move to San Francisco years ago, but he had already shipped out on a tanker when they finally arrived. He knew that they probably had written him off as a rambling wastrel, but he decided to ask for help. After sixteen years, he knew without putting it to the test, that they'd not send plane fare to any city but San Francisco. They sent him a family ticket and he'd showed up at their home just two weeks before, with a stubble, a wife, a child and a pocket full of bills.

"*Michael Granahan!*"

Mike looked around at the nurse and decided that she, too, could be described as "*crisp, starched and efficient,*" and he grinned, not because of his game with off-stage editors, but because it gave him a tremendous kick to hear the baby's name called, as if he were supposed to answer. He toyed with the fantasy of seeing the baby swivel around in his snow-suit and say, "*Down, Pop, that's 'junior' she wants. That's me, she's calling. Like, man, isn't she the crisp, starched and efficient doll, though? They tell me a lot of broads really dig us premature types.*" Mike took the baby from Angie as she stood up and they followed the nurse into the cubicle. She pointed to the examining table and said, "Undress him completely." She looked at Mike and asked, "Are you his father?"

Mike hesitated and thought: *Here comes that grandfather bit,* but he grinned and said, "No, I'm his mother." The nurse looked blank and said, "The doctor will be with you in a minute." Mike felt himself flushing, and as she went out, he laid the baby on the table and started undressing him. Angie laughed and said, "Here, let me do that while you rehearse another routine. That bit just laid a big fat eggeroo." She leaned over Little Mike and said, "If I ever thought you'd inherit your old man's taste for corny comedy, I'd walk off and leave you right here. Now I know where your father lost that front tooth."

The baby seemed to react, smiling, as his little crossed brown eyes darted around, focusing on nothing.

"I hope he doesn't get cranky in front of the doctor. I want him to make a good impression."

Mike started to say something about doctors being accustomed to dealing with cranky children, but stopped. He realized that he, too, wanted his only child to make a good impression on the doctor, on the world. He remembered Little Mike as he had first seen him in the incubator, a little bundle of raw meat, huddled in a corner. He remembered his own first reaction, which was something akin to horror. He knew that other fathers must have had similar reactions, but he knew that not many fathers had waited as long as he had for a child, only to discover that a newborn baby looks more like a chicken or a kitten. Now, at nine months Miguelito did look like a baby, even though he was not doing many of the things, other full-term babies could do.

"This is Michael?"

Mike looked at the doctor and was startled at his youth. His name-plate read: Dr. SILVERSTEIN, and Mike felt that this made his youth seem less important. To a kid from the Bronx, even an Irish kid, the words "Jewish Doctor," have a reassuring ring. He smiled. "Yes, this is Little Mike, and I mean 'Little.' He was only seven-and-half months." The doctor just nodded, and Mike thought, *I wish I'd saved that "I'm-his-mother-bit" for this guy.* He fell silent as he watched the doctor run his hands all over the tiny body. Little Mike seemed to enjoy this and tried to focus his eyes on the doctor. As the doctor measured him with a tape, one of the children in the corridor began to cry. Little Mike's face puckered and he started to wail in a nerve-wracking monotone. The doctor took an ordinary safety-pin and rubbed it along the baby's feet. He increased the pressure, but Little Mike paid no attention to this personal problem. He seemed concerned only with the misery of the child in the corridor. After a few moments, the doctor looked up.

"Does he cry like this often?"

"No. Only when he hears other children crying." They had answered simultaneously and in such perfect unison, that Mike was embarrassed, but he managed to smile.

"How do you like that glee club effect?"

The doctor didn't smile or answer. He opened a folder on the small desk in the corner of the cubicle and said, "I'm sorry there's no place to sit, but I have a few questions to ask about Michael."

The questions involved the circumstances of Little Mike's birth and seemed routine enough, but Mike was aware that he was growing uncomfortable, and he could not attribute this solely to the baby's whining or the doctor's evident lack of humor. He found himself denying that the baby was a fussy eater or that he was given to crying unnecessarily. The young doctor seemed not so much to be asking questions as making statements that were virtually accusations. Mike did admit that *occasionally* the baby was a feeding problem, but what can one expect from a baby that could not yet hold his own bottle? And it was perfectly true that the baby never cried except where he heard a siren on TV or in the street, or when other children cried within earshot.

Angie described the baby's delivery, her own prenatal condition, and a few comments from nurses and doctors on the O.B. staff, while the young doctor wrote interminably. Angie had become uncomfortable, too, he noticed and her voice had taken on a pitch that he recognized as her "I-know-you're-not-going-to-believe-this" tone, and the whole scene became strange. Even in his unnerved state, he was aware that he was able to commend himself for not having described the scene to himself as "Kafkaesque." He found himself getting angry at the young doctor, who seemed to him to be the anomaly which created the atmosphere of tension.

He's stupid, this kid, he thought, *and nobody named Silverstein should be so humorless, either. It's ... it's ... un-Jewish!* He realized at once how stupid his own reaction was and how ridiculous his own choice of words, but the cubicle had become stifling. Little Mike had changed octaves, and Mike suddenly had an almost uncontrollable urge to grab the baby from the table and run with it to some safe haven where there were no crying children and no stupid, poker-faced medical students masquerading as pediatricians. He fought the urge as Dr. Silverstein stood up, closing the folder.

"Well, you are fortunate to be in San Francisco," he said. "We have all the facilities to follow these children and advise their parents. I'm going to refer Michael to Dr. Thelander, who is an expert in this field, and she'll know how to help this little fellow with his problems.

Mike relaxed a little and the scene started to return to normal. Angie zipped up the snow-suit, a difficult maneuver, since Little Mike never cooperated. Mike thanked the doctor, who merely nodded, but without a smile, and already opening another folder as Angie and Mike gathered the baby up and left the cubicle.

Doctor Thelander's office was in a new wing of the hospital and Little Mike stopped crying as soon as they were out of earshot of the crying child. They had both relaxed, and Angie was chattering to the baby again.

"We are going to get you some real action, now. We're going to build you up, my dear little Banana, so you can compete with those other bananas in the bunch back there." The baby groped for his mother's face, his little eyes rolling in his head. "We can probably make you Top Banana. Your old man's losing his grip." She turned to Mike, grinning evilly. "That doctor didn't think much of your act, did he? Neither did that nurse."

Mike chuckled. He was happy again, and he rubbed noses with the baby, simultaneously squeezing Angie's hand. "Don't worry, Little Banana, when we get you filled out and teach you a few dance routines, I'll take you to an agent I know. He's always looking for talent, and any son of mine is bound to have talent. If I ever thought you'd wind up working for a newspaper, I'd eat you right now!" He pretended to bite off the baby's nose.

"Stop, you're frightening him!" Angie held him close, protectively and melodramatically. "Touch not my child, you . . . you ogre!"

"Frightening him? Why, the Granahans are absolutely fearless. We're all descended from Irish noblemen and bartenders, which is, of course, a redundancy, and we pay homage to neither God nor man. Even the smallest of the clan, even those yclept *Little Banana*. Even those members of the clan with Mexican Passports."

This was one of the things they shared, but whose importance they would never admit openly to each other. The baby had to have a passport to leave Mexico, and the document had become a treasure. It was always missing from its last resting place, but neither would admit having moved it. Mike had come upon Angie on one occasion, holding the baby's tiny thumb print to her cheeks and gazing into the future with misty eyes. He withdrew quietly, and she never knew he had seen her. He himself had taken the passport off to some corner on a few occasions, and marveled at the wonder of it all. He'd had a son after all these years, and the little rascal had to carry his own passport! He took a sort of pride in the fact that the Mexican government had seen fit to acknowledge the existence and importance of his son. He delighted in reading his son's measurements in meters and thinking of his little crossed eyes as being *"Color de ojos . . . Castano."* It sounded so much more distinctive than "Chestnut." He had, on a few occasions, left the passport lying around the apartment when they had visitors, and then taken care to point out that the little bundle cooing in the crib was a full-fledged Mexican citizen. Mike himself had never had a passport until he was twenty-five, and he tried to picture Little Mike's passport twenty-five years hence, with a picture of a sturdy young man with clear straight chestnut eyes and a large thumb print. Mike could enjoy dual citizenship until he was twenty-one, and then he would have to choose one or the other. Mike would let him choose for himself, hoping that passports would not be so important two decades hence. In any event, when little Mike was twenty-one he would be a man and quite capable of deciding such important issues for himself, if his parents gave him a set of values and allowed him to think for himself. The baby's future was in their minds at all times, but although they talked baby-talk and acted as silly as newlyweds, they never discussed the passport in any but the most unsentimental terms.

As they crossed the lobby, bringing Little Mike to one of the first steps on the long road to his Future, they came to a ramp, instead of a stair well.

"Down here, I guess," said Mike, swinging the baby over his head making him giggle. He saw a nurse coming up the ramp and whispered in the baby's ear, "Crisp, starched and efficient."

"Down here to Doctor Thelander's office?" he asked her.

The nurse smiled. *Oh,* thought Mike. *Frosting on the cake. Crisp, starched and efficient and SMILING!*

Then she spoke.

"Yes, the Cerebral Palsy Clinic. The extreme end of the corridor." At the words, the strength went out of his arms and he clutched at the baby and slid him down to his chest. He held him tightly, too tightly and the baby grunted. *Oh, my God,* he thought, wildly, *this has gotta be a mistake! Not the Cerebral Palsy Clinic! Not for Little Banana! Cerebral Palsy Clinics are some kind of fund-raising gimmick.* He looked after the nurse desperately as she moved up the ramp, wanting to call her back, call her words back, explain that he was a jobless newspaperman with an only son and people, especially nurses, didn't say things like that to a man in a situation like this. *Cerebral Palsy Clinics are for other people. Cerebral Palsy Clinics are for rummage sales, not for Little Mike! Cerebral Palsy Clinics are where distraught parents bring their twisted, crippled and retarded children! They're not places where you bring a chestnut-eyed little bundle of joy, not a Little Banana with his own passport!*

He felt Angie's hand on his arm, and he was sure she must feel the ice in his veins. Her voice was far away, and he thought at first she didn't understand, because she said, "Then we can't miss it, if it's right at the end." Then he saw her face. Her mouth was slightly open, and she was wearing an expression he had never seen before. They were moving slowly down the ramp and Mike's thoughts went out of control again. *CEREBRAL PALSY! He* was the master of the cliché, the virtuoso of the euphemism, the guru of the gag, and the words "Cerebral Palsy" were like a kick in the groin. All the words he had learned to live with, "premature," "a little slow," "under-developed" all seemed to be words from a language he no longer understood.

They saw the sign: DOCTOR FRIEDA THELANDER— CEREBRAL PALSY CLINIC, and he felt Angie's hand tighten on his arm. He turned to her insanely.

"That crisp, starched, efficient son-of-a-bitch was the only one who *smiled* at us all morning!"

Angie didn't speak or react in any way, and Mike opened the

door wide as though he were expecting machine-gun fire and he wanted to get it over as soon as possible. They entered and stood in the middle of the room, trying to adjust to its contents, as though stepping from darkness to light, or light to darkness, for this was also a roomful of children and parents, but they were *different*. Here was the blind child throwing a tantrum on the floor. Here were the twisted, misshapen children with that *look* in their eye, and here, finally, were the parents who were middle-aged in their twenties.

A receptionist said, "This is Michael, I guess."

Mike thought, *that nurse we met on the ramp must have brought his folder down.* Angie smiled and said, "Yes, and he's had a long, busy morning." Mike recognized that voice and that smile. It meant she was putting up a front, and he fell in love with her all over again.

They found a seat and watched as the blind boy finished his tantrum and pushed himself along the wall in a sitting position. They tried to make small talk with the other parents, and tried, with difficulty, to keep from staring at the more afflicted children in the room. None of the children were crying now and Little Mike snuggled up in his father's arms contentedly, as though he knew, at last, that he was among his own. In his anguish, Mike thought of that line from the Rubaiyat: "*What, then, did the hand of the Potter shake?*" He was a little surprised to discover that the words seemed to cheer him slightly. Then he remembered from experience that when he was able to indulge in little dramatizations of his catastrophes, his ship would not sink completely.

He kneaded Little Mike's body gently in his arms, and rubbed his chin over the little fuzzy head and tried not to think of Little Banana's Future. He seemed so tiny and so normal among these older, more grotesque children that Mike was grateful for the Present.

"*Michael Granahan!*"

Mike could not recapture the pleasure he had felt previously when they had called his son's name, for here were many children, and maybe Mike would be one of them, who would never answer to their names, no matter what mechanical devices were used on their twisted bodies.

They entered the office and undressed the baby again. Dr. The-lander gave him a thorough examination. They didn't speak until she looked up and said, "You knew, of course, that Michael was a brain-damaged child?"

"Oh, yes!" They had answered again in complete unison, neither willing to admit that they had just been dealt the cruelest blow of their lives minutes before on the ramp. "I guess we sound like a glee club," said Angie.

Dr. Thelander laughed. "A little flat though," and they all laughed. "We want you to become very active in the parents' group, and we'll do everything we can for little Michael."

When they left, Angie's purse was full of brochures, and her eyes were unnaturally bright.

"Can we afford a cab? It's . . . it's kind of a special occasion."

"No, we can't but it is a special occasion."

In the cab they were silent for a moment. Little Mike slept soundly in his father's arms. Suddenly Mike was contrite. "You know, Dr. Silverstein thought we *knew*." Then he added, slowly, forcing himself to speak of the subject that would occupy so much of their thoughts for years to come. "God, it's hard to think of Little Banana as . . ." he hesitated and rejected several euphemisms, dragging the specter into the light, ". . . a backward child."

Angie faced the specter and tried to smile, in an effort to be equal to the occasion, and said, "Well, his parents aren't so FRONT-ward!" But the effort was wasted for immediately they were both crying, and a loud sob from Angie woke Little Mike and he started to whimper.

The cab driver looked in his rear-view mirror at the trio united in anguish and pursed his lips. He started to speak, then merely shrugged, a gesture that most closely resembled a shudder, then turned down Divisadero toward Pine, driving much faster than the traffic laws allowed.

Kevin Costello is the pseudonym of Gerald Aloysius McCann, short story writer, journalist and playwright. Mr. Costello has held editorial posts with publications in Mexico City, Ft. Worth, San Francisco and other cities. He is the director and founder of the Pacific International Press Service. His short stories appear in numerous magazines.

"I remembered the old saying,
 'The fuller the pockets, the taller the man.' "

When Money Talked to Me

BY ROY WOLPER

**A cheerful, down-to-earth account
of lessons in life styles.**

AT least once every month, I take Carroll Susan to the Totem
Pole. Carroll Susan would rather go to a movie with me or sit in
front of her fireplace and play Peggity or listen to records while
lying on the braided rug in front of the sofa. She says the restaurant is expensive and that I never enjoy my dinner (and she knows
how hard I work for my money).

But that is why I go to the Totem Pole—the high prices. I, too,
would rather have a quiet evening—walking through Highland
Park in the snow and holding the thumb of her mitten and going to
her house and the large kitchen, which we imagined was *our*
house, for hot milk with its sweet skin (even Carroll Susan likes it
this way now)—but I go to the Totem Pole because there money
can see who is boss—money or me.

If I were eating a two-fingers thick steak at the grocery store that
my Uncle Andrey and my father and I own (they gave me one

third the summer before my senior year in high school, for they knew that I had worked well and liked the store), money could say, "Your're a hypocrite, Boruch. You have a thick steak, yes. But that's because you get it wholesale." But when I go to the Totem Pole and spend five dollars on dry white chicken breasts or on lean tight roast beef without gravy, I can say, "Money, I'm boss."

More than once I've explained all this to Carroll Susan, but she doesn't believe money talks. She has never had enough money for it to talk to her, and it never talks to me when I'm with anyone. Carroll Susan is intelligent and logical, and she calls money's talking a Russian superstition.

But it talks.

On a summer night two years ago, my father told me about money's talking. Our store was closed. Uncle Andrey had gone home and my father and I were in the little kitchen back of the store, eating. I was sitting on an empty pop crate. My father was in the big chair, eating braunschweiger-and-swiss-cheese sandwiches with potato salad. I don't like cold meat; I had broiled a rib steak for myself.

"It will talk to you," my father said, after he had eaten half his pickle. My father doesn't speak English well; his *w*'s come out *v*'s, and he frequently puts in a Russian word, and so I will write his words better than he says them. "You are young. In school. But no matter. Money will talk."

"Money talk?" I said, thinking he was teasing me.

"I've been watching you all year." The way he said it—looking at me all the time—told me he was serious. "Tonight you changed Mrs. Kolura's oranges from a twenty bag into a ten. To Mrs. Haspell you took lemons out of a number five and spilled them over her cans. You save bags."

He made a sandwich by folding one slice of bread in half; it was so thick the cheese hung out. "You're close. You'll have money. Then it talks." He began eating, but he kept talking: "It didn't come to me in Russia. Only here, after our store got healthy. Then it came. It will come to you."

"When?" I had to put the piece of steak back on my plate and cut it again. It was thick.

"Maybe next week," he said. "Next month. Maybe next year." My father ate the potato salad with his fingers. "You have money, don't you? You've been saving it, haven't you?"

"Yes," I said, answering both. With school, I worked the evening and Saturday and Sunday. But in the summer I had been working all day and every day. And I had saved my money. I did not know Carroll Susan then (we met that fall when she came to our school and was in my history class); and I had never gone out with anyone else.

"Then money will talk," he said. "Or maybe sing. Or talk and sing together. But," and he tapped his fingers on the heel of the rye bread, "you must not listen."

"I won't listen," I said.

"It's easy to say it. When money's not talking."

"I won't listen," I said.

There was no more potato salad and no more meat or cheese. He ate the last slice of the rye bread by itself. "If you listen, you're done for." As he stood I was surprised how small he was. He punched my chest, a little punch. "A good night, Boruch."

"Good night," I said, and I called after him as he went up the stairs to our apartment, "I won't listen."

As I pulled the light cord and snapped the bolt on the door and checked the lock to make sure that it had caught, I believed that I would not listen.

A little less than a year from the day my father had talked, money spoke. It spoke on my seventeenth birthday, July 2. Every year, on my birthday, I put my worth into my notebook. I wrote, *Age 17, Net Worth $4,782.14.*

I leafed back to the first page, and I saw that when I was thirteen, I was worth $72.19. Underneath in careful and thick letters I had printed, *When I have $150.00* (and I had never thought that day would arrive), *I will buy a Ford Sedan with a heater and a compass and snow treads.* Snow treads meant prosperity.

When I was fifteen, I was worth $689.79. I had money for the car and snow treads but the money had come in so slowly I did not spend it.

At sixteen I was worth $1,212.11. But I was still getting a salary then. I was not an owner.

Now my net worth was $4,782.14. That was a lot of money.

"More money than most people your age have," said money to me. His words were quiet, respectful.

"I worked for it," I said. "Hard."

"Yes," said money.

"Seven days a week," I said. "Except for school, and then I work at night."

"Yes," said money.

"Others went to football games. They went swimming the days when it was so hot I thought my shirt was part of my skin. I'd shut my eyes, and I'd see the water at North Park, blue and cold and fresh-smelling."

"You worked hard." From the way money spoke I knew it understood the long hours and hard work of a grocery store. "Now," said money, "when you walk past men your own age, you can spit in their eye. No more Ford sedans. A Cadillac."

There was a silence. I could hear the night wind at the glass, but inside the room there was only stillness and money and me. Then money said, talking so low I just could hear the words, "But you could have had more."

"How?" I said. "I work twelve hours a day. I'm so tired—some nights—I fall asleep with my clothes on."

"Yes."

"I couldn't have worked harder."

"Listen," said money. "Last Wednesday night you took Carroll Susan to the Nixon Theatre. That cost eight dollars and fifty cents. You two ate first. Another seven dollars. Fifteen-fifty."

"It was her birthday," I said.

"Fifteen-fifty more." And money said, "You had five steaks last week."

"They're not expensive. I get them wholesale."

"Thick," said money. "Each week. Nothing's wrong with steaks, but there are thinner ones."

Money went on, "Tonight you had a milkshake at Abernanthi's. With two extra scoops of ice cream. And malt. During the year you've had one hundred and forty-nine milkshakes."

Money was quiet. It had spoken firmly. It knew my life.

"How much could I have had?" I was curious.

"Close to seven thousand dollars," said money. "Eighteen hundred dollars difference. Boruch, think about it."

During work next day I sorted money's words and looked close at them. My Uncle Andrey said to me, "Is the mule sick?"

"No," I said.

"You've been unpacking this one carton for five minutes," he said. "All day you've been walking like the sick. Go home if you're sick."

"I'm not sick." I tried to work harder, but I was not able to, for money's words were turning over in my mind.

At night, after I was in bed, money came and asked, "Boruch, how much do you make on a loaf of bread?" Money talked quietly, the way my Uncle Andrey walks.

"Four cents," I said. We sell it at twenty-two cents a loaf; it cost eighteen cents.

"Forty-five thousand loaves of bread have to be sold for eighteen hundred dollars," said money. "How much do you make on a quart of milk?"

"A penny and a half," I said. Milk is like bread—every customer knows the price, and the profit is low.

"One hundred twenty thousand quarts of milk," said money. "A lot of milk."

"A lot of bread," I said.

Money said, "Think it over, Boruch."

The next day I could not keep money's words from my thinking. At dinner I did not eat well. My mother's lamb stew was good, but money's words had filled my stomach as well as my head. Even the tea—which I like to have at the end of a dinner—did not taste as good as usual.

After my mother saw that I had stopped, she said, "Enough?"

"Yes," I said. I did not talk to my mother—not because my mother is not intelligent, for she is—but because money could never speak to my mother.

After I had closed the store that night, I tallied the register for the amount of business. It had not been a busy day. There was not much money and not much profit.

I thought how hard it was to make money. I kept thinking of that as I went upstairs and into my room. I was sure money was close by, and I said aloud, "Money, you are right. Money is hard to make. To hold. I have been a fool."

"You're not a fool," said money. "You just made mistakes."

"Eighteen hundred dollars' worth of mistakes," I said. "A lot of bread and milk," I said. "Money, you are right."

Tuesday was busy. The next night, after my night class was over, I went to Carroll Susan's. Usually we would go to the Totem Pole restaurant; the dinner with white tablecloth and candles and with Carroll Susan sitting next to me was one of the two high spots in my week. The other one was Sunday when I took Carroll Susan out for the evening.

When I called for her, she looked beautiful with a black dress that matched her long hair. I wanted to take her out and show her off and add to the world's happiness, but as I said good evening to her parents, I remembered the words money had spoken to me, and when I talked to Carroll Susan, I made sure to tell her that my work earlier in the day had been hard. I said I was too tired to have a nice dinner. "If we go to the Totem Pole I'll get home late. Tomorrow will be impossible for me," I said.

We did not go. We each had two hamburgers and coffee at the Big Boy Drive-In. They were large hamburgers—the forty-five-cent size—but still hamburgers.

That night, before I went to sleep, I heard money say, "Boruch, well done." His words were like a pat on the back, and I felt good.

During the hot days I did not stop at Abernanthi's for a milk-shake with two extra scoops of ice cream and malt. I went straight from the store to my bedroom. Abernanthi saw me on the street a month later and asked what was wrong. I told him I was tired of milkshakes. "You could come in and say hello to Abernanthi," he said; "I like you." I told him I would stop in soon.

But each night I went straight home. Often that summer money came up to my room and said to me, "You're doing fine, Boruch. Keep it up."

Infrequently I took Carroll Susan to dinner, but on those nights I didn't order dessert; I made excuses as easily as if money were whispering advice in my ear. We went to neighborhood movies instead of the ones downtown. We took long walks and went for rides in my car and spent hours on the swings at the playground; all of these were free.

One night, before the arrival of fall, money said, "Best year yet, Boruch. You're ahead of most seventeen-year-olds. Head and shoulders."

I remembered the old saying, "The fuller the pockets, the taller the man."

"Thank you, money," I said. "I feel the growing inside me."

"You still have loose ends," said money softly. "Little things." He said louder, "But you are coming along fine, Boruch."

In bed, as I was going to sleep, I thought about the little things. I had believed I was doing a very good job of saving. I began to think of ways of tightening up.

I re-used a razor blade for an extra shave. I did not get a haircut every second week; I got one every three weeks and saved more money. Carroll Susan and I watched more television.

Before I went to bed at night, I would stand in front of the mirror, and I was so tall in my eyes that I filled the glass. "Hard work," I said to myself. "And saving."

I got into bed and lay on my stomach (I sleep best on my stomach) and many nights I heard money whisper the same way my mother had talked when I was sick: "The pockets get full. And more full."

Before I slept, I often felt so tall that I could have, if I had wanted to, reached up and taken hold of the moon.

The end of November, the pianist Shearing came to the Totem Pole and Carroll Susan reminded me that I had promised to take her to hear him. Shearing's music is like the magic of the stars or the air.

I told Carroll Susan I was not feeling well—that I had a little pain in my side—and so we watched an old movie on television. We had popcorn and hot milk before I went home, and although the popcorn was buttery and warm, it was not sweet. As I ate, and later as I drove home, I had the feeling that the popcorn knew my smallness. And maybe that's why it was not good.

After I undressed, money came beside me and said, "Well done, Boruch. I'm proud of you."

"I wanted to take Carroll Susan to see Shearing," I said. "I had promised her."

"You were right to save five dollars," said money. "Maybe another four dollars for the little things."

I was glad money had come to my room and was supporting me. I had really wanted to take Carroll Susan to the Totem Pole.

As I put on my pajamas, money kept talking: "You did the right thing, Boruch. Your pockets are full. You are taller."

I heard, and I wanted to believe. But something was wrong with money's logic. I should have taken Carroll Susan to hear Shearing. It would have made her happy—and me.

As I stood in front of the mirror, I did not feel proud or good. I looked at myself. I was not tall. I was a small Boruch.

I do not know when my father noticed, but in the first week of December—in the afternoon while I was at the meat block cutting a steak for myself—he said, "That for you?"

There was nobody in the store. I said, "It's for me."

He walked over to the block and felt it. "Thin."

"I'm not very hungry," I said. I did not pay for the steaks; but if I ate a thin one, I would have the big ones left and we could sell them for more money.

"You weren't hungry yesterday."

I had not known that he had seen me cut the steak the day before. I said, "No."

"The day before that?"

"I wasn't hungry either," I said.

He looked at me. "I remember the days you were always hungry."

I didn't answer.

"Did it talk about bread?" he said. "Milk?" He was not angry or disappointed. "Did it tell you about spitting in a few eyes?"

He was standing so that I had to go around him. I did not answer right away. Then, because he was my father and I had to tell him the truth, I said, "It spoke. I listened." Without looking at him, I went on, "It showed me how much my milkshakes had cost. And steaks—the thick ones. Taking Carroll Susan to the theatre."

Three customers came in. Before we went to wait on them, my father took me by the arm. "Remember tonight. Bookkeeping night."

I nodded. The bookkeeping of the store was my job, and one night a week I went over our accounts.

After the store had closed, I posted the week's bills to our ledger; it was a slow task because to compete with supermarkets we had many credit accounts. As I was ending my work, my father came down and sat in his big chair and we went over the accounts of the week. After we finished, my father said, "My stomach's hungry. How about us eating?"

"All right." I sliced a steak for myself. He cut one two-fingers thick for himself. He picked up the steak I had cut. "Thinner than this afternoon."

I put the two steaks in our broiler.

When I didn't answer, he said, "I must talk with you, Boruch." He was looking not at me but at his hands, and he moved his fingers as if he were sorting his words. "Soon you must choose. Who is Mister Boss? For keeps. You or money."

"I'll soon be at school," I said. "Only here in the—"

"Don't slip away from me," he said. "You or money."

"The more full the pockets—"

"So what if the man is little," he said. "I am little."

"After awhile," I said, "I'll be boss."

"After a while," he said, "it is worse." He pointed his fork at my steak. "Next year money says no steak. Two slices of chopped ham. Soon it says ham is expensive. Eat bologna." Bologna is the cheapest meat.

"Then you can't be boss. Even if you want to." My father was pushing the steak about with his fork and talking. "Save your

153

money. Spit in two eyes. Maybe ten. That is important." He stopped, and he pointed his fork at me, "Boruch, remember you never get a day back. No thick steak tonight, tonight is gone." He put his fork down. "People, too."

I stood and walked to the meat block. The rib was still out. I cut a steak as thick as my two fingers. I went back into the kitchen, holding the steak. My father did not talk for a while—until after I had cooked the meat and had put it on my plate and started to eat it. And it was good—the way a thick steak is good.

For a little we sat there, and then we began to laugh for nothing was as funny as me, Boruch, having six thousand dollars and shaving with old razor blades. I told my father how crazy I had been, and we were laughing so much tears came into our eyes. Then we had our tea.

After I was in bed, money came and said, "Boruch, I'm surprised. You loosened the pockets." Money went on, sharply: "I thought you were more intelligent."

"I was wrong. Foolish," I said. "And you caught me. Not any more. Ever."

"Listen to me," said money. I rolled onto my stomach. But money went on: "You only think you're away from me, but you'll save a nickel here. Fifty cents someplace else."

"I can spit in your eye."

"Listen to me, Boruch," said money, but money's talk did not go into my ears.

Shearing had gone, and so I took Carroll Susan to the Totem Pole. We each had five dollar roasts that my mother or Carroll Susan's mother could have made better. My roast was so dry that I could not finish it. And then I thought about the tip for the waitress and for the checking of our coats, and I began to whistle. And that is something, for I can't whistle or sing well.

Carroll Susan did not understand.

Even now, after we have gone to the Totem Pole a half dozen times, she does not see why we do not go to a play or to a restaurant that I might like. If I did that, money, who is always around, might think that the pleasure was worth the cost.

But he can't think that when we go to the Totem Pole. There I spit money full in the eye.

Born 1931 in Pennsylvania, Roy Wolper grew up in a family-owned grocery store. He has his Ph.D. in English literature and teaches at Temple University. He is the co-editor of an eighteenth century newsjournal, The Scriblerian. *In addition to short stories (many about Boruch and his family), Mr. Wolper has published essays on Samuel Johnson, Voltaire, Swift, and others. In 1974 he won a National Endowment for the Arts Fellowship.*

"... you can look at his forehead
under a microscope, but you'll never discover
his secrets."

Guests from the Province

BY ARKADY ROVNER

**Fantasy and mystical experience—
the visibility of secret thoughts.**

ANATOLI Gavrilovich Orlyashkin was very fond of his name and patronymic and also of his last name. His given name was of antique Roman origin: Anatoli. His patronymic was even more ancient and honorable; his father's name was Gavriel, like the archangel, therefore he was called Anatoli Gavrilovich. His last name was likewise not ordinary: it derived from "orel" which meant "eagle." One encountered it rarely, not like the usual Tarakanov, Averanov, Svistynov.

He could enumerate all the heroes whose names were like his, all the writers, and artists and even high government officials. Whether he was listening to the radio, watching television, or reading some newspaper—from every side his namesakes and others who bore variations of his name reached out to him. He rejoiced in their fame and success as he would have in his own.

When he heard, for example, how the woman who was reading

the evening news on television pronounced his first name, his heart was rinsed in a warm bath; he would feel very well, meritorious, and he would summon his wife from the kitchen.

"Olga! Olechka! Did you hear? Anatoli Yegorov has just been designated Honored Artist of the RSFR!"

Or, the next night,

"Gleb Orlyashkin has just made right wing on the Red Army Soccer team!"

And one day he even heard on the news:

"Anatoli Gavrilovich Orlyashko, deputy president of the Something-or-Other Union—"

"Oh, for heaven's sake!" His wife raised her hands in mock annoyance as she peered from the kitchen. Her fingers spread wide and wet, and glistened with onion-skin scales and meat crumbs. She brushed her hair from her forehead, but her face still couldn't be seen, only her glossy plump neck.

Anatoli Gavrilovich's wife was kind and compliant. She always kept a bottle for him in some secret place at home, so that he wouldn't drink somewhere else, on the sly with his friends, in the park, or at work, or in doorways, and end up arrested. She hid bottles of vodka in the corner behind the hall mirror where it stood on the table, or in his faded raincoat in the vestibule closet where he could reach in and feel the bottle deep in the pocket. And Anatoli Gavrilovich was always ready to indulge in his favorite occupation.

But Anatoli Gavrilovich scarcely drank any more. Previously, he used to drink seriously, until he got ill with the shakes, until he began to hear voices. He used to know how to drink. But now only one bottle of vodka was sufficient to tumble him into bed.

His wife set no obstacles in his way. Therefore they lived together as if their two souls were one, as if they breathed with one breath, with tenderness, love. He would call her Olenka, she would answer Tolenka; he would call her Olehik, she would answer Tolchik; he would call her Olyusheehka, she would answer Tolyushechka. And at night, while certain things were occurring in bed, she would murmur his name in various melodies: his stomach would tickle inside him with pleasure.

Anatoli Gavrilovich respected his wife highly.

And yet, at the same time, he did indulge himself in certain thoughts. On streetcars, in the stores, he would spot some girl whose skirt ended several inches above her knees—she had to be slender, her eyes must be large—and he would approach her and fondle her, to probe her all over—to remember it all afterwards was impossible.

Or he would line up a dozen young girls in a row, undress them, and bestow attention on each in turn: one girl he would pat on the fanny, he would caress the breast of the next, another he would honor with greater favors.

Or else—but here he was especially afraid he might give himself away—he would look for some boy to live with him, to act as a husband to him. And whomever he chose, he lived with, and even paid the boy well.

To carry on like this in real life—Anatoli Gavrilovich was too lazy, too cowardly. But he kept all these alternatives in his head for variety. These—and others, many others.

He would be sitting at a table, for instance, drinking tea, or at the office rustling papers . . . But this was only for show, because during these moments his thoughts were in fact far away. After all, it isn't forbidden to think. Likewise, someone else's thoughts can't be known. You are sitting across from someone, you can look at his forehead under a microscope, but you'll never discover his secrets.

Anatoli Gavrilovich had yet another secret; he believed in God. He knew that from the scientific viewpoint God didn't exist, and yet he believed, because upon occasion he would feel such splendor in his soul that he needed no other joys. And he liked to ponder how the world is constructed, and what is occurring therein, and what omens are offered to help a man understand. Anatoli Gavrilovich could find some significance in everything, even in the least incident: for example, whom he met on the street, how they looked at him, and what color were the passerby's socks. He took note of all this, weighed it, and determined his whole life's direction therefrom. Should he, for example, do a certain thing right away, or wait, and see how things would turn out by themselves?

He imagined God to be a bird who walks in the sky, balancing on one foot and the other, in search of nourishment. Sometimes the bird flew down to Earth and revealed secret omens to him, Orlyashkin. He immediately registered these omens, but did not share them with anyone. However, he noticed that after thinking of God, inside him there was suddenly light and tranquility instead of the usual murkiness. And after such mental entertainments, his forehead would be covered with sweat and his head heavy, dark, and the blood would beat in his skull. But all the same, he couldn't restrain himself from this particular folly.

Anatoli Gavrilovich was very concerned that his thoughts not become visible, and therefore liked to give an impression of strictness. He was a man of position, of significance, of reticence, so sternness became him.

Thus one day—it happened toward evening—Anatoli Gavrilovich was sitting on the sofa in his new corduroy slippers, sent from the Crimea by his wife's sister, watching television on his set which was, incidentally, the very best label.

On the yellow scatter rug right next to the television there undulated and moaned a girl of about twelve, her clothes ripped, hair dishevelled. Anatoli Gavrilovich had noticed her earlier from his office window. Her small white socks lay helplessly on the floor beside the yellow rug. Also present was the pimpled youth with murky eyes who lived on the next floor; Anatoli Gavrilovich usually stroked his head when they rode together on the elevator. Both of them, the boy and Anatoli Gavilovich, panting and sweating, were tearing apart the convulsive girl on the floor. Her tanned legs were beating the air over their heads.

The occasional direct kick of the soccer ball through the goal posts, the hero responsible for which feat unfailingly seemed to bear Orlyashkin's name, from time to time relieved the tensions of the bloody occurrences on the yellow rug. Anatoli Gavrilovich quacked with satisfaction and once more returned to the interrupted enjoyment of his current preoccupation. The girl was no longer crying, she only moaned quietly.

He was perched on the sofa, tense and pale, his lips trembling, eyes cloudy, hands sweating. Just then the doorbell rang. Such a light and quiet ring . . . repeated at quick intervals, but with a delicate touch.

Stealthily wiping the sweat and trying to make himself breathe more evenly, Anatoli Gavilovich went to unlock the door. He opened the door and saw a man standing on the threshold: a man of small stature, with his head beside him. Anatoli Gavilovich's eyes darkened at the sight of such a wonder. Only later did he realize that the man's neck was twisted laterally, and therefore his head appeared to be off to one side.

Suddenly the head began to whisper to him—the face didn't move at all, only the lips on the side of the face were opening and closing.

"And I know about the girl, and I know about the boys. Give me a bottle of vodka or I'll denounce you to everyone."

Anatoli Gavrilovich was stunned. Without a word, he opened the hall closet, flung himself at the faded raincoat, and not even looking at it, pulled out the untouched bottle. He thrust it in front of him in the open space and convulsively slammed the door, and then hurriedly turned all the locks with shaking hands. "Who was that?" his wife called from the kitchen.

"Nothing, a mistake," Anatoli Gavrilovich answered in a strangled voice, and darted like a mouse past the kitchen door on into the bedroom.

He was alone. For a long time he couldn't gather his thoughts, nor clamp his senses back together again. He switched off the television: the room became quiet. But in the kitchen, the water was gushing from the faucet making a horribly shrieking sound. But he didn't go to turn it off, because he didn't want to encounter his wife. He sat down on the sofa. He jumped up. He sat down once more.

"And what if he really tells people? What will happen then? I'll be blackballed everywhere. It will be the end."

As these thoughts sank into him, something tilted inside, and he had to hold onto a chair to keep his balance.

"But how could he have found out? Not one living soul . . . Thoughts, purely thoughts! After all, they couldn't have leaked out anywhere. Or did they?"

Anatoli Gavrilovich was tortured with doubts.

"After all, anything is possible. And now Crook-Neck will start coming here every day for vodka, as if he were going to the store . . . In any case, necessary and timely measures must be undertaken. Otherwise it will end badly. But what can be done, what can I think up?"

Plans began to collect themselves in his head one after the other.

"Maybe to treat him nicely, to bribe him? Or to threaten him? And what if I were to silence him with an iron pipe—I'd wrap it in a newspaper, as if it were a bottle of vodka—he wouldn't have time to dodge! And then carry him to another floor, leave him there, and who would find out?"

Anatoli Gavrilovich continued to muse along these lines for the rest of the evening. The fear inside him would pull in his stomach, or push up into his throat, and in the end it wrapped itself completely around him like his old raincoat.

When he began to fall asleep, he saw himself behind a very long table which was standing in the middle of a field. A bird was walking around the table, hopping from one leg to the other, always watching him from the corner of its red eyes. And from the far end of the table a head was rolling toward him. As it rolled closer, and he recognized Crook-Neck's head, with its lips moving at the side of the face, Anatoli Gavrilovich jumped out of bed and screamed.

Olga paddled barefoot from the kitchen, bringing him a glass of kvass. He drank it, felt better, and fell asleep as if he had plummeted through a hole in the ice.

In the morning Anatoli Gavrilovich felt constricted, stiff, gloomy, as if the weather inside him were overcast. Even asleep, his head was aching with a metallic hangover—from sobriety— and he tried not to awake until the pain faded. It was Sunday, his day off. Outside the window birds were chirping, the sun was shimmering through the window, and his wife could not be heard in the kitchen. She had gone early to market.

Anatoli Gavrilovich poked his feet from under the blanket, thrust them into his slippers, sat up, and remained sitting there, staring ahead in a stupor at the dark rectangle of the vestibule. His thoughts were rattling like iron bars in the dark space of his morning consciousness.

"God, how awful! God, I'm sick! Nauseated. Why do I feel so lousy? Everything is awful. No escape. Nausea, nausea rises and stays in my throat. And what in the world do I lack? I've got a wife, and a good apartment, and God didn't skimp on the television set either. So what? Everything's trickling away. Everything's useless. Nothing helps. You play with everything, as if these toys mattered. And now what? Boredom. Disgust with everything. Something inside me is yearning, pining, for what I don't know. I feel such melancholy—I could tear out my hair, scratch my face till it bled, bang my head against the television. Or better yet—roll on the floor and howl like a hound . . .

"But what can you do? You don't want to howl. And you don't want vodka. And you don't even want some new girl."

That is, perhaps he could have had a drink, and he could have patted the fanny of some naked little girl, and he might even have found some interest in that, but this wasn't the heart of the matter. And if they offered him some other debauchery, maybe he would have responded in the usual way. But Anatoli Gavrilovich saw in all this the special finger of God: there was meant to be nothing around him that could distract him from his main preoccupation.

And his present thought concerned an elastic band.

It turned out that life itself was an elastic band. You hold both ends and pull. While you are holding on, pulling it—it seemed necessary to do this. But the minute you let go—you can't possibly remember why you have been holding it taut for so many years. On this elastic band are drawn: your honor, and your situation, and your God. Everything's there. You let go—and there is nothing. And then what is left?

Here Anatoli Gavrilovich began to think hard. If both God and all those girls were only tensions within the mind, then everything else was likewise only deception, mirage, soap bubble. And then—Crook-Neck also didn't exist!

The doorbell rang.

Anatoli Gavrilovich's heart leapt, then plummetted, smashing a hole in his guts. Hands trembling, he dressed, tiptoed to the vestibule. He clasped his hands together to quiet their shaking. His legs also refused to obey, and he stood leaning against the hall closet. His heart had gotten lost somewhere down there, nor was it beating at all now.

He slowly turned the lock and with eyes of glass peered through the crack in the door. Two men stood on the threshhold. Crook-Neck was not with them. Their faces were stern. One held up a sheet of paper.

"Orlyashkin, Anatoli Gavrilovich?" he asked in a hollow voice, glancing from the paper to the fraction of Anatoli Gavilovich's face visible through the crack. "Collect your things: you're under arrest."

"What for?" Anatoli Gavrilovich croaked, and froze.

The men, however, took their time in answering. They kicked open the door and pushed past him into the room. Anatoli Gavrilovich followed them in confusion. The guests sat down side by side on the sofa, and the one with the paper read aloud:

"You are accused of the murder of Citizen Crook-Neck by means of an iron rod on the stairs in front of the door of your apartment."

Suddenly Anatoli Gavrilovich felt desperate.

"How do you know? What evidence do you have?" he shouted, comprehending that according to the order of things there could be no evidence. "And who are you anyway?"

Then he saw how his guests' faces grew stupid. One of them scratched his leg, the other thrust his finger in his nostril.

"Okay, Pop, we were just kidding. Slip us a bottle, and everything will be all right. Otherwise—you know what will happen."

Anatoli Gavrilovich was prepared to be as frightened as he had been the previous day, but he noticed that something was wrong. What—he didn't understand. The one thing that was clear: he musn't give himself up, but on the contrary, become even more aggressive with them.

"Who the hell do you guys think you are? I ought to take you to the police—they'll show you a thing or two!" he shouted and loomed over the men on the sofa. At first they just waved him away.

"Don't bother, let's not talk about the police. No point in it. Your local threats don't concern us. We're from another province."

"From what province?" Anatoli Gavrilovich gathered strength from his own anger, and waved his hands, even trying to graze them in passing. "Blackmailers! Sons of bitches! I'll show you how to crash into people's apartments and frighten them!"

And here's what happened: the men shrivelled up, retreated before his waving hands. Anatoli Gavrilovich merely grazed one of them with his fist, and both men fell at his feet as if dead and lay there.

And Anatoli Gavrilovich was again ready to take fright, but he realized there wasn't a moment to waste. No time to wonder or ponder what had happened. He carried the men out as fast as he could, one after the other, dragged them to the floor below, and left them.

Glancing around, cold sweat trickling, he stole back upstairs three steps at a time to his own apartment and noiselessly locked the door behind him. He undressed quickly, plunged into bed, and covered his head with the blanket.

He lay for a long time in the dark. However much he tried to calm himself, his whole body continued to tremble. Nor did the trembling diminish. Any minute they could ring to inquire about the murdered men.

"But what did they want?" he kept thinking, curling up tighter under the blanket. "What do they want, what are they after? And who are they—Crook-Neck and the two others? From what 'other province,' to what were they alluding?"

Nor could Anatoli Gavrilovich explain his easy victory. Out of habit, he would have liked to discover some omen in their appearance. Soon, however, he understood that this wasn't just a sign, but something which threatened to overthrow all of his life as he had known it.

"Maybe Death was my guest?" he thought suddenly, turning to stone. Anatoli Gavrilovich was very afraid of Death, and didn't like to think about it. He knew that "there," if "there" indeed existed, everything would be different than here, and this was too terrifying to ponder calmly. The only thing he craved now: to live as he had lived before, before Crook-Neck. How comfortable, how much in balance, everything had been! In balance with what— Anatoli Gavrilovich didn't know, but he knew that everything had been thus before.

And what about his restless thoughts? Well, who lives in peace with his own thoughts anyway, within his own imagination? After all, no one does. He was convinced of this because he himself was able to smell out other people's lechery from a distance. What was this? Did this mean that Crook-Neck called on everyone? This isn't according to the law, nor should it be. This meant, then, the visit was a mistake, an infringement of the rules. And if it was a mistake, then who could lay a hand on him, Anatoli Gavrilovich Orlyashkin? According to what law?

These thoughts made him feel warmer, but still unsure.

Anatoli Gavrilovich emerged from the blanket and tiptoed around the room. He switched on the television. The room filled up with cheerful marches. He clapped his hands and began to dance like a Cossack in front of the mirror. Then he paused to stare sternly at his reflection, and smiled with satisfaction.

At this point Olga his wife returned from market and slapped her heavy baskets on the floor. Anatoli Gavrilovich and his wife Olga Illarionovna lunched. After lunch Anatoli Gavilovich read the paper and again watched television. No one disturbed him about those two men. Supper with vodka and zakuski-herring and salmon and pickles and marinated mushrooms—and his calm was quite restored. He felt strong-hearted and even frolicsome. He clowned around, didn't let his wife squeeze past him into the bathroom, and afterward crawled under the table, bleated and made faces. And he and his wife roared with laughter and danced around.

Their gaiety was interrupted by the doorbell.

Anatoli Gavrilovich went to open the door, swiftly sobered. He looked out: six men stood on the threshold. Their faces and clothes were identical. They grinned, and one of them asked:

"Are you Orlyashkin?"

Born 1940 in Odessa, Arkady Rovner spent most of his life in Moscow. He is a graduate of Moscow University (philosophy major) and is now working toward a doctorate at Columbia University. In Moscow he was an editor and translator at the Academy of Social Sciences. In 1975 he "left Russia because of the restrictions on creative endeavors." Since then his short stories have been published in the USA, West Germany and other European countries, in both Russian and English. He is the editor of Gnosis. *His translator is Elisavietta Ritchie.*